OPEN WATER

POL ROBINSON

2011

Bella Books, Inc.
P.O. Box 10543
Tallahassee, FL 32302

Printed in the United States of America on acid-free paper
First published 2011

Editor: Katherine V. Forrest
Cover Designer: Linda Callaghan

ISBN 13: 978-1-59493-229-8

Dedication

To the Olympians among us; both the Special and the able-bodied. You embody an ideal to which we all aspire.

For Sheryl.
Always.

Acknowledgments

Longfellow wrote, "*Look, then, into thine heart, and write!*" A moving directive, to be sure, but a writer can only get so far on heart alone; the rest comes from research, from community, from family. The following are representative of those who contributed directly or indirectly to this project: various rowing clubs across the country for providing invaluable information on their websites on terminology and proper technique; members of the Radlist who responded so positively to the original short story; NaNoWriMo for the impetus to hit that tantalizing 50k bar; and the GCLS for the tremendous community and opportunity that splendid and growing organization offers readers and aspiring authors. Additionally, my online families—the Bella Forum and GateWorld especially—provided cheers and spurs as needed.

Thanks to athletes—both active and armchair—and coaches at all levels. Credit for this project goes to Gypsy who said so long ago, "You should do this," and to Sheryl who said emphatically, "You *can* do this." Extra special thanks to Jeanne Magill for expeditious first and last readings and marvelous critiques. I am so grateful to Linda Hill, Katherine V. Forrest and the Bella team who have been so supportive and welcoming. Last, but by no means least, thank you to my family: Sheryl, Matthew, Megan, and Charlie (the wonder dog). Without your love and support (and enthusiastic tail-wags), this book would not be... and neither would I.

Prologue

"Just lie still."

"Where am I?"

"You're at St. John's Hospital, you've been in an accident."

Blurry, indistinct faces floated in and out of her line of sight. A cacophony of sound battered at her senses, pulling her focus from the words coming from the mouth at her ear. There was something she needed to know, something...

Later, the voice was back.

"Cassandra, we're going to have to take you to the operating room. Is there anyone we can call?"

No, there's nobody. I don't have anybody. Cass tried to get the words out, her grief at just those few words darkening her face. Finally she forced out, "M'leg. What's...I can't feel my–" Even that effort cost her and she collapsed back against the bed.

The voice hurried to reassure her, "I know it hurts, honey, but we have to call someone."

"Nobody...nobody to call," she mumbled, trying to clear her head of the haze. *My leg. Oh my God. I can't...no, it's just not there.*

Cass fought back panic and tears. She felt her throat close up and she began to gasp for air. It was over. She'd be lucky to walk again, let alone get into a boat to row. She blinked up into the light, turning her face away as the mask slowly descended. Voices around her raised as she fought to stay away, desperate to know what was happening.

"Please," she whispered into the clear plastic mask. "Please don't take my leg."

CHAPTER ONE

"Ladies and gentlemen, we will now begin boarding United Airlines flight 8460, bound for Beijing. Passengers holding tickets..."

Cass jumped as the woman's voice boomed out of the speaker just above her head. She tuned out the rest of the boarding call as she flipped her book closed and patted her pocket for her ticket. Around her, the general hubbub of voices grew as people came to life with the boarding call, everyone gathering their bags and extras and moving to stand in line. Cass watched the odd sampling of humanity that made up her fellow passengers begin to crowd to the gate.

Why is everyone so eager to stuff themselves into a tin can? We'll be in that thing for nearly sixteen hours. What's the rush?

Taking advantage of the announcement to stretch her legs one last time, Cass slipped her carry-on over her shoulder and moved to the window and gazed at the huge silver aircraft. *Nose, two wings, lots of engines...top floor, windows for the pilot to see out of... looks okay to me.* Cass watched as a tall blond woman in a dark blue uniform chatted with a scruffy-looking member of the ground crew. The man, wearing bulky kneepads and ear protectors, laughed at something the woman said, then gestured toward the rear of the plane. He looked up at the uniformed woman, then made a note on the clipboard in his hands. The woman peered over his shoulder and nodded sharply; then, taking the clipboard from him, she patted the man briefly on the shoulder and began to walk around the plane.

"Ma'am?"

Cass turned to find the loud gate announcer at her elbow. Her polyester uniform ironed to a shine, the woman eagerly reached to take Cass's arm.

"Ma'am, if you'll come with me, we have your boarding pass all set up."

"Um, I think there's been a mistake, I have my boarding pass here..."

"No, ma'am. We are overbooked and had to make some changes." The gate attendant glanced around conspiratorially, then lowered her voice. "See, the captain is a fan and saw that we were overbooked and then noticed that you were in coach, so..."

Uh-oh. Shifting her feet, Cass pulled her arm free. "Uh, fan? But...I'm not anybody." *What, does the guy think I'm some gullible actress?*

The woman tugged again and Cass planted her feet. "Look. No offense and, um, tell your captain I appreciate it, but I really don't like taking those kinds of favors." *No telling how I'd have to "pay" for the upgrade. No thanks.* "Tell him that—"

"Her."

"What?"

"Her. Captain Landers is a 'her.' Or I should say, Captain Landers is a 'she.'" The attendant cocked her head slightly, then suddenly smiled at Cass. "Oh, honey, it's not like *that.* The skipper's just a former rower, er, 'sweeper' I think she called it. Anyway, she was tickled when she saw your name on the manifest." She patted Cass's arm and shepherded her to the gate, past the long line of now-curious passengers. "C'mon dear, you let Cecelia handle things, okay?"

Amused now, Cass followed Cecelia down the ramp to the plane, listening to her chatter about how Landers was an "almost national" sweep-oarsman a few years back and how she, Cecelia, had never heard of sweeping before—aside from the whole broom and dirt thing—but now they, the whole San Diego-to-Beijing crew, knew all about Cass and how she was joining the team late and they were all sending her their wishes for her success in the upcoming Games. Just listening to the woman wore Cass out and she was glad when she was handed off to the flight crew.

"Hi, Cassandra Flynn?" Barely waiting for Cass's nod, the new attendant quickly ushered Cass into first class. "I'm Meredith, nice to meet you. Wow, the Skip is so excited! You know she used to row for Cal, right? She said to tell you that if you don't mind she'd like to come out and chat with you sometime during the flight, is that okay?"

Like Cecelia, Meredith barely paused for breath, seeming to expect nothing more than the occasional nod in response. Cass obliged and settled into the spacious seat next to the window, letting the perky Meredith stow her carry-on bag above her head. After another minute or two of excited gushing, Meredith took off to help the other passengers settle in, leaving Cass to her "peruse the safety card" preflight ritual.

"That won't help much, you know."

The low voice in her ear surprised her and Cass looked over her shoulder to find a pair of laughing blue eyes, framed by the gentle crease of lines that traced a face that had seen its share of the sun. *Oh my, what have we here?*

The eyes belonged to the body Cass had seen earlier on the tarmac, encased in the blue uniform and walking around the plane. The body straightened and Cass was forced to tip her head back to maintain eye contact. Tall and blond in that "I'm Swedish and proud of it" way, the newcomer was at least six feet tall by Cass's guess; she would easily top Coach Thompson's five-foot, nine-inch frame. Cass guessed the woman was about twenty years her senior, somewhere in her late forties or early fifties. Her dark blue uniform was pressed to within an inch of its life, the razor's edge creases of her trousers breaking evenly just above her shined shoes. The care taken to look sharp spoke volumes to Cass about the woman wearing it. Broad shoulders decked out in five gold bars bespoke her rank, as did the marks on her sleeve identifying her years of service. She stood leaning gently against the back of the seat in front of Cass, one arm casually draped along its top. Cass let her eyes drift again to the face above her, unconsciously returning the easy smile she found on the tanned face, enjoying the mischief that lurked in the bright blue eyes.

Cass herself, at five foot three, was on the short side for a sculler, especially a double sculler, one of only two in a boat. She could see from the reaction that she was not what the captain expected.

Captain Anne Landers stepped forward and grinned down at Cass tucked comfortably in the first-class seat before her. Small and made even smaller by the large leather seat, Cass Flynn did not look like an Olympic-level sculler. She looked more like a co-ed on her way home for the term. Anne knew, however, that looks were deceiving. Packed into that small body was the equivalent of a small package of dynamite. Soft brown eyes sparkled up at her under a mop of curly brown hair that reached just past her powerful shoulders; shoulders that Anne knew could propel a shell through the water at an amazing speed. Yes, Cass Flynn was tiny but mighty, as her own partner might say. Landers knew it was cliché, but she couldn't resist, "You're much shorter in person. Do you get that a lot?"

Cass raised an eyebrow in response, then her grin mirrored Captain Landers'. "How's the weather up there, Stretch? Do you get *that* a lot?"

Landers threw back her head and laughed heartily, drawing looks from the boarding passengers; one man not-so-subtly nudging her as he moved past. Ignoring him, Anne stepped into Cass's row and asked, "Mind if I sit for a minute? It's getting kind of crowded in here."

Shrugging one shoulder, Cass tilted her head to the empty aisle seat next to her. "Sure, be my guest. It's your plane, right?" Cass's gaze traveled from the Captain's shoulders down to the hash marks on her sleeve.

Anne followed her glance and smiled again as she caught Cass's final look at her left hand. "Yup, it's my plane and yup, I'm married...or as much as the government will allow." She waited, her smile growing as Cass caught her meaning. "Not to worry, this isn't some awkward pickup," she reassured Cass. Landers looked again at the safety card in Cass's hand and gestured with her chin, "I was not kidding about that card, by the way. As high as we'll be, that little bit of paper won't be much help."

Cass's gulp was audible and she slid the emergency procedure pamphlet back into the seat holder. "Uh...great. Well, thanks so much for stopping by, I feel *so* much better now."

The captain chuckled as she stretched out in the seat, watching as the remaining passengers shuffled aboard carrying everything from large bags to small animals. Shaking her head as a man wrestled what appeared to be a cello down the narrow aisle, she returned her attention to the woman next to her. *Cass Flynn is on my plane! Janie's gonna freak when she hears. I've got to get her autograph without sounding like a complete dolt.* In her college days, Anne had been a skilled sweep rower, one of eight on a crew, but she had been nowhere near good enough to make the national team. Her partner, Jane Zimmerman, had been a member of her college's eights crew, but she too had missed the cut for anything beyond that level of competition.

Anne and Janie were still avid followers of the sport, however, and Anne was still trying to get Janie an open berth on a partner airline so they could catch the heats together live in Beijing. She couldn't believe her luck today when she'd spotted Cass's name on the manifest for this, her last flight before her vacation began. After checking the rest of the manifest, Anne had called the gate crew, and made a simple request. She did not often ask favors of the crew and Cecelia had been happy to make the change she requested. A few keystrokes later and Anne Landers found herself seated next to one of the best scullers in the country.

Cass studied the woman who had planted herself in the seat beside her. Presumably, this was the mysterious "Captain Landers" who was responsible for her bump up to first class. Up close, she could see the laugh lines that framed the bright blue eyes and their matching partners around the edges of her ready smile. As the flow of passengers began to slow, Cass, remembering her manners, cleared her throat and stuck out her hand. "Hey, thanks for the upgrade, I appreciate it. I'm Cass Flynn."

"Oh Lord." Anne stuck out her hand. "Anne Landers and you're welcome." Anne clasped Cass's hand in a cool, firm grip. She grimaced slightly as Cass's eyes widened. "I know, not *the* Ann Landers. To quote somebody, I am Anne with an 'e,' and that makes me, um, not her." She chuckled as Cass grinned back at her.

"And...well, she's dead, isn't she?"

"Well, yeah, there's that, too."

Cass waited as Anne paused and scratched her head. "So, in case you haven't figured it out yet, I am a huge fan of yours. If you don't mind, can I pop back during the flight to chat a bit?"

"Sure. But, um...don't you have to do that 'flying' thing?"

"Nah, it kind of flies itself, really. Besides, Jim can take care of the in-the-middle bits. I just do the up and down bits."

Again Anne paused and Cass wondered why. The captain had made a special effort to make her more comfortable and now seemed hesitant to talk to her. Finally, Anne spoke up again. "Look, if you need to rest, or are tired, or, whatever, it's really okay. I can—"

Cass shook her head. "No, really, it's great. Ah, Cecelia said that you used to row?"

"Yes, I—"

Meredith's voice came over the loudspeaker, interrupting Anne's answer.

"Ladies and gentlemen, if I can have your attention for just a moment..."

"Crud." A small frown crossed her features as Anne pulled herself out of the seat and glanced into the flight deck while

Meredith began her preflight recitation over the intercom. "Okay, time to get to it. I'll pop back later. Really, though, if you're tired or have things to do, just do them. I won't bug you." Despite her assurances, Cass sensed that the self-assured captain felt awkward about intruding.

Charmed by the older woman, Cass gently teased the pilot, "Great, I'd love to hear how it was in the old days."

Anne's loud, throaty laugh filled the cabin again as she brushed her trousers straight. "Old days!" She snorted again with laughter and tossed a last smile at the brunette grinning up at her. "Fine, youngster, I'll be back to bother you later."

CHAPTER TWO

Cass sighed and readjusted the pillow at her shoulder. The takeoff from San Diego had been uneventful and the flight the smoothest she could remember in a long time. Unfortunately, rain had obscured her view of the ground after takeoff, depriving Cass of the chance to see the training center from the air. As she often did when flying, Cass let her mind wander, trying not to focus too much on what awaited her at the end of her flight. The thrill of it all was there, though, tucked away safely. Every once in a while she would let herself revel in the idea that she was going to the Olympics. The Olympics! A dream since childhood, it had faded with time. Even taking up rowing in graduate school had not really reawakened the dream. It was a fantasy, really. What team would want a nearly thirty-year-old athlete with no proven records? No solid international standing?

Returning to college eight years after getting her bachelor's degree and being bitten by the rowing bug soon after, Cass had found herself in a world far different from the one she had experienced as an undergraduate. Discovering a gift for research and a love of a sport she'd always longed to try, she had thrown herself into both. Standings or rankings did not matter; she was not really trying for any team. She had just needed something to take her mind off her studies for a while, something that would keep her fit and allow her some time to relax. Rowing seemed the perfect sport.

On a whim, she had gone to open tryouts for the University of Wisconsin team and nobody had been more surprised than she when she'd made it. She had tried several events before finding her niche as bowman in the double scull. By the end of her attendance at UW-Madison, Cass had her master's in kinesiology, two National Championship medals under her belt and her eye set on the U.S. Rowing Training Camp and the Trials. One late night at the library, combined with a rainy drive back to her apartment, had brought those plans to a screaming, painful halt. She flashed back to that night, letting the pain of that moment fill her. Because it was that pain and despair that had driven her so hard to come back.

Cass slowly swam back to consciousness, pushing through the miasma of medication-induced haze. The first sensations to penetrate were smell and sound. Hospital. She was in a hospital. The unmistakable antiseptic smell brought her further to the surface, accompanied by various sounds. As she became more aware, she began to categorize the sounds. The beep of the monitor above and behind her, the squeak of soft-soled shoes on waxed floors, a murmured conversation just outside of the door. With consciousness came increased awareness and...pain. Cass gasped and tried to reach down, anxious to know.

"Shh, honey. Don't move."

Blinking groggily, Cass turned her head and found the owner of the voice. A nurse was bent low over the rail, clearly trying to get Cass's attention. "You awake now, honey?"

"Mh-hm." Blearily she blinked again, trying to bring the woman more clearly into focus. She tried again to reach down. She had to know. "M-my leg?"

The nurse's expression froze and with it Cass's heart. She briskly twitched the blankets around Cass's body straighter, her face grim. "I'm sorry. We called your...family."

Cass opened her mouth and then closed it again. She was terrified to ask. She could feel her leg, could feel pain. But, she'd read too of phantom pain and was certain that this was what she was feeling.

"The doctor will be in to talk to you."

The look of pity on the woman's face was almost too much for Cass to take. As the nurse stepped around the bed, Cass finally managed to ask, "How much did you take?"

"Of what, honey?"

"My leg."

"Oh, no. No, no, dear. It's all there." She hastily moved back around the bed and patted Cass's shoulder.

"I...it...it is? But," Cass gaped sleepily at the nurse, trying to decipher the anger and pity she saw on the nurse's face. "But you...what are you sorry about?"

Her jaw set, the nurse turned her face away for a moment, then turned back again, her gray eyes almost fierce as they captured Cass's gaze. "I'm sorry honey...the university gave us your family's number." The nurse looked uncomfortable. "Your aunt and uncle. They said they won't be coming. But," the nurse pasted on a falsely bright smile. "They wish you well."

Watching the clouds slide by below her, Cass struggled to push the memories aside. She knew the nurse had added that last part to be kind. Uncle Marty and Aunt Lisa had not sent their good wishes, of that she was certain. She shook her head as the unwanted memories crowded in.

One of those "get it there in an hour" pizza guys had gone right through a light and into the side of her little car. During her recovery Cass had heard the nurses talking; it had taken the on-scene medics and firefighters more than thirty minutes to free her from the car. Days in the hospital, weeks in rehab recovering strength and feeling in her leg. A double-compound fracture they had called it. Even the words sounded harsh to her. She had not cared what they called it. All she had known was that the damage would likely ruin her chances to row again.

It had taken a year—a year of the hardest work she had ever done. She had recovered from the initial surgery well, surprising the doctors with her ability to heal. The rest had been up to her. Hours of physical therapy, both supervised and unsupervised, had paid off. She had persisted despite cautions from her doctors and her therapists. Again her thoughts drifted.

"What's the rush, Cassie?"

Cass scowled at the physical therapist assigned to her. She hated being called Cassie, especially by this woman, who had the manner of... well, she couldn't really think of a good simile.

"C'mon, Cassandra, you're pushing too hard. It's not like you have to train anymore, right?" The slightly mocking, condescending tone grated on Cass's nerves, fueling her drive to work harder.

"Look, Marta, why don't you buzz off? I'm working here. I meet with the doctor on Monday and if she gives me the okay, I'm back in the shell."

Anger clouded the face of the therapist and Cass couldn't help but react. She and her therapist had mixed like oil and water from day one. It was clear that Marta disliked working with her as much as Cass dreaded their sessions. She had overheard Marta asking to swap clients, but since this was her last student clinical rotation, she had not been successful. They were stuck with each other.

"Fine. It's not like you're ever going to compete again. Good luck with your paddling." With that parting shot, Marta had huffed off and that was the last Cass had seen of her. Her words had done the opposite of what the therapist had planned, Cass was sure. She'd driven herself harder, determined not to quit.

As the drink cart rattled past, Cass pulled herself from her memories. This was why she hated long flights. Too much time to think. She'd been driving herself so intensely she'd been too exhausted to think. She yawned and stretched, feeling the familiar pull of the tight skin of her left leg.

Three days, ten workouts and one doctor's appointment after that therapy appointment and Cass was lowering herself into a beat-up practice shell with the help of Danny Thompson, UW's assistant coach. Danny understood her need to get back into the shell, the drive and need to return to some sort of normal life. Cass did not hold any illusions that she'd be able to compete at any level again, she had just...*needed* to get back into a shell, to get back to something in her life that felt real to her. She had to prove, at least to herself, that she was not the quitter her mother was. That her aunt and uncle had repeatedly told her she was.

Aside from the driving need to prove herself, Cass had simply missed it. The water. The shell. The...all of it, really, even the exhaustion of training hard. Several times during her self-imposed training and after a long workout, she had rowed herself out to the middle of Lake Mendota and just lain back, the oar handles carefully balanced in her hands, the blades turned and resting flat on the water. Gently pushing with her legs, she would slide the seat back in its track, stretch out and watch the storybook clouds float lazily across the sky, accompanied by the faint buzz of insects and the gentle slap of water as it danced along the hull of her shell. It was in those silent moments that she'd heard again that call for competition. Felt that pull.

Danny had patiently paced her, pushed her and yelled when she'd needed it. Most of her friends had left town after graduation, headed off to new jobs and new lives with their new degrees. Cass stayed in Wisconsin, recovering from her injury and contemplating pursuing her doctorate. The insurance settlement by the pizza company and the driver's personal coverage made it possible, if she was careful, to concentrate on getting back into shape without other distractions.

Despite it being too late to be a part of this year's Olympic Games, Cass had thrown herself into her training. Even now, she was not sure why she'd felt that driving need to get back into shape. Whatever the reason, she had pushed herself and it had paid off. Eight months after her release from the hospital, Cass was back on her game; her race times equal to, or faster than, before her injury. The night Sheila Adler, head coach of the U.S. Women's National Rowing Team, phoned her and asked her to attend the training camp in San Diego was one Cass would never forget. The days between that call and getting on the plane to China had passed in a haze of frantic activity.

Six weeks of grueling training at the ARCO center in San Diego had made those lonely weeks of recovery and solo work at home seem like a waltz. An easy one. Heat after heat after heat against some of the best young collegiate athletes in the country had made Cass aware of every year she had on those women. But every ache had been worth it. Where they had youth and vitality, Cass added maturity and experience. And an unrelenting drive to win.

The rumble of the drink cart in its return journey again brought Cass back to the present. *Enough*, she decided. *That's past. Now is...now.* Smiling to herself over her not-so-profound philosophy, she pulled out her laptop and reviewed what she knew about the women she'd be joining in Beijing. Coach Adler had told her when she'd called to ask her to join the team that Amy Lindquist, coxswain of the eights crew, would be her roommate in the Olympic Village. Other than Amy, whom she'd met only briefly at an after-regatta dinner just days before her accident, Cass did not know many of the squad members well... Really, she only knew three or four and that was by reputation only. The rest of the team had been through the training center months before and they were already in Beijing prepping for the Games. She wished some of the team had been back in San Diego...at least her rowing partner, Sarah. It was going to be hard enough to fit in with a tight group of women, let alone learning to mesh her style with that of the other woman in her boat.

Putting aside her nerves at both the prospect of fitting in with an unknown group of women and the upcoming regatta, Cass opened the secret little door in her heart for just a moment. *I am an Olympian. I am going to compete in the Olympics.* Carefully controlling her excitement again, Cass settled into her seat and gazed out at the ocean below. She'd been over the moon when the coaches told her to pack her bags for Beijing, that she'd made the cut. She'd made her dream come true and she'd prove to them all that she could do it.

CHAPTER THREE

Moaning and sweating, Laura Kelly reached blindly in her sleep, her hand lifting off of the sheet only to fall limply at her side, fingers twitching. "No," she mumbled, then turned over restlessly.

Sheila Adler stood in the doorway of the little dorm room and considered her options. She was in a bind and needed someone to make the trip to Beijing Capital International Airport to pick up the team's newest member, Cassandra Flynn. All of her assistants were out on the water or in the gym today, and Sheila had just been asked to coordinate a meeting between visiting parents and sponsors, and she had to attend. That left her with few choices. Laura Kelly was the Captain of the U.S. Squad and stroke of the eight-boat; making her the next logical choice for Sheila.

On the bed, Laura moaned again and lifted her hand again,

as if to ward off attack and Sheila shook her head. She wondered how long the nightmares had been going on. Maybe it had been a mistake to not assign Laura a roommate. When Laura moaned again, Sheila stepped forward and carefully rested a hand on her arm.

"No! I didn't mean it! I—" Laura jerked awake with a gasp.

"Shh, Laura. Shh. It's me, Sheila." Sheila gave Laura a gentle shake, keeping her hand on her arm until the green eyes focused on her face. Slowly the wild-eyed fear began to slide away, replaced by the carefully blank expression Laura so often wore.

"Okay?"

At Laura's nod, Sheila stepped back and sat on the chair opposite the bed. She watched Laura scrub her face and take a few breaths, giving her athlete time to settle.

"I came by to ask if you'd make a run to the airport to pick up the newbie."

Clearly still shaken by her dream, Laura shook her head. "Can't one of the assistants go?"

Sheila tilted her head and studied Laura, watching her shake off the last of her nightmare. *She should have been too tired to dream*, Sheila thought. The way she'd been pushing herself since they'd transitioned to Beijing. First into the gym and the last out, first onto the water and last off, Laura should have been too exhausted. Maybe it was time to reconsider her approach. She knew what Laura had been through in the last year and thought that letting her work off that pain and stress in the gym and on the water would be the best way, but now...now she wondered if she'd done the right thing. Noting the dark circles and lines under Laura's eyes, Sheila decided she hadn't, and now was as good a time as any to change. She shook her head. "Nope. I've got everyone out today with the singles and quads and I can't spare an assistant. The trainers are all over at the new site checking the new medical facility. I've got a parents and sponsors meeting. Come on, Laura. I want you to do this."

The coach waited as Laura stood and stretched, once again appreciating the magnificent physique of her lead rower for the big boat. Laura was in fantastic shape, at the peak of her physical conditioning. It was up to Sheila to see that she remained that way for the upcoming regatta, physically *and* mentally.

Laura stretched again and blew out a long sigh. She met Sheila's gaze for a long moment and then turned to pull fresh clothes from the small dresser nearby. "Yeah, okay. Can you write down her flight stuff for me? I'm gonna grab a shower."

"Sure." Sheila stood and turned to leave. She stopped Laura on her way to the bathroom with a hand on her arm.

"Laura?"

"Yeah."

Everything about Laura screamed "don't touch me, don't ask me," but Sheila did anyway. "I'm here if you need to talk, okay?"

"Yeah. Sure."

Laura pulled away and closed the bathroom door behind her, leaving Sheila staring after her, wondering when Laura would ever forgive herself. Or if she could.

CHAPTER FOUR

A sudden drop in cabin pressure made Cass's ears pop, startling her out of her restless doze. She looked around, confused for a moment. *Oh yeah...plane...Beijing...Olympics.*

Cass shifted in her seat, taking advantage of the extra room to spread out. Her unexpected bump to first class had had an added bonus—the space next to hers was empty, allowing her to spread out over two seats for the nonstop flight from San Diego to Beijing. Cass had been too excited to sleep on the first part of the flight. Later, she and Captain Landers had talked crew every chance the pilot had, Landers sharing her experiences as a sweep rower two decades earlier. Sweep rowers were typically bigger than single- or double- lightweight scullers like Cass, and Landers certainly fit the type. Cass had obliged the pilot's request for an autograph, blushing the entire time. They had said goodbye midway through the flight, with Landers heading back to the flight deck and Cass trying to snatch a few hours of sleep.

God, I am wiped. Cass stretched again and leaned her head against the cool window, hoping to catch a glimpse of something below her other than water. No such luck. She had fallen asleep almost immediately after Landers left, taking just enough time to recline the sleeper seat before letting her eyes slide shut. Now, with the nauseating up-and-down movement of the plane, Cass was suddenly afraid she was going to be sick. It was very apparent that she would not be getting more sleep any time soon. She struggled upright and quickly reset the seat to its normal position, hoping that would help. It didn't.

Cass clenched her jaw as the plane dropped again. Around her, other passengers groaned and mumbled in discomfort. Sternly ordering her stomach to stay put, Cass rustled around for something, anything, to distract her. *Evacuation procedures... not a good thought, techno-widgies for sale...no thanks...*

"Bag?"

Cass looked up to find the air steward beside her seat, imperiously waving a bag over her head. Grateful, she nodded and instantly regretted the movement as it just added to the sickening rise and fall of the plane. She snatched the airsick bag from his hand and clutched it to her chest, hoping to ward off the inevitable.

The attendant continued moving forward, his crab-stepping effort to stay on his feet reminding Cass of an old-time sea captain moving from stem to stern in tossing seas. His supply of bags was dwindling as green-tinged passengers followed Cass's example.

Another rise, another dip and more groans filled the air.

Cass fingered the bag she had gotten from the attendant. *Clever, it looks like a film bag. Huh, they are even advertising Kodak film!* Cass wondered if the advertising was to disguise the bag's purpose. For a moment she panicked. *What if he gave me a film bag! It is not gonna hold anything. Oh crap!*

I do not get airsick!

I.

Do.

Not.

Get.

Uh, oh...

With a gasp, Cass surrendered. Head bent, eyes closed, she lost what little she had been able to eat of the excellent meal they'd served in the first-class cabin, praying that the film bag would hold. It did. Mostly. Amazingly, once she was done, she began to feel a bit better. It helped that the flight seemed to get a bit smoother.

Cass carefully sealed the bag, then called the attendant to her seat. While she waited, she searched her carry-on and grabbed the only spare clothes she had handy, a pair of soft, worn shorts. She briefly lamented her lack of any official Team USA gear, knowing that it waited for her at the end of her flight. Cass brushed again at her now damp legs. She knew trying to wash the remnants of her airsickness off her jeans wouldn't work very well while in flight and there was nothing worse than sitting in wet jeans, so a quick change was in order. She was somewhat ashamed at the little bit of pleasure she got at the look on the attendant's face as he took the bag gingerly between two fingers. *Oh yeah*, she thought. *Don't think I did not feel the plane suddenly level off as I finished losing my dinner. I'll bet you were all placing bets up front, eh? Yeah, old 5C tossed her cookies first! Let's hope my luck holds in China!*

CHAPTER FIVE

Cass tucked her passport back into her bag as she pushed her luggage cart through the teeming mass of people. Her leg was aching from the long hours of inactivity and she was walking with a slight limp, trying to loosen the muscles. She maneuvered the cart to one side of the flow of humanity, searching the crowd hovering around the entrance. How the heck was she supposed to find anyone in a crowd this size? She realized suddenly that she wasn't entirely certain she'd be able to spot Coach Sheila if she saw her. She'd only seen the coach's photo once, in the team biography. Great. Searching the crowd, Cass shuffled to one side as an overladen baggage cart zoomed past.

Another wave of arriving passengers surged around her and this time Cass let the swell push her forward. She tried to steer to one side of the swirl of eager travelers, her limp more pronounced following a blow by an elderly woman's bag. Cass stepped up onto the bottom ledge of the cart, trying to get a better view of the faces waiting behind the white-roped line. Through the crowd she caught a flash of red and white before the crowd shifted slightly, blocking her view. Stretching high on her toes, she leaned to the left a little and saw a face she vaguely recognized. She waved and the woman cocked her head, then lifted a hastily scrawled sign reading, "Flynn," her expression questioning. Cass nodded and grinned, then began to steer her cart across the current of incoming travelers. She didn't think the woman holding the sign was the coach, but at least she was holding a sign with the correct name.

Cass lost sight of the sign-bearer for a moment and growled in frustration. This was nuts. She stepped up again on the bottom shelf of her cart and craned her neck around, ignoring the complaints of her injured leg. A flash of sea green caught her as she connected again with the woman in the "Team USA" T-shirt, holding the sign with her name. Their gazes caught and held. Cass felt her breath catch and, for an instant, forgot her frustration with the crowd. The blazing depth of those eyes holding her own shot through Cass, reaching deep inside. For a single, blinding instant, Cass ached. Then, just as quickly, the green eyes shuttered and Cass was set adrift. She shook her head and hopped down, then, determined to cross the remaining crowded stretch between them, tried the approach everyone around her was doing. Just...push forward. It worked. The crowd around her parted and she found herself face-to-face with the holder of the battered sign. Cass reached around the cart and stuck out her hand. "Hi, I'm—"

"Flynn?"

"Um, yes, I'm Cass Flynn. It's—"

"I'm Laura. You're late, let's go."

Without another word, Laura spun on her heel and headed toward the door, leaving Cass staring in open-mouthed amazement.

Welcome to Beijing.

CHAPTER SIX

Cass stumbled as she tried to keep up with Laura's long-legged strides. The woman had barely said two words to her after meeting her plane. Laura's abrupt greeting and subsequent departure was an unpleasant surprise. Especially after... *Especially after what, Cass?* For a second, when she first spotted Laura, Cass had felt...something. A sharp tug inside as she'd connected with the green eyes of her new teammate, then it was gone. *You are tired and you are imagining things.* Laura was rapidly drawing away from her as she threaded her way through the crowd toward what Cass assumed were the exits. The airport around her buzzed with activity, people hugging, kissing, laughing and crying. Some doing so all at once. Slamming to a stop to avoid a bright-eyed five-year-old future Indy driver and his luggage cart, Cass lost sight of her companion. She used the cart as leverage as she looked for her, then sighed as two of her bags slid off the cart and landed with a thump at her feet.

Well, crap.

Bending to pick up a bag, she was stopped by a pull on her sleeve.

"What is the matter, my friend? Lost already?"

Cass turned to find Captain Landers at her side. She smiled tiredly up at the pilot. "Well...sort of." She looked around again, trying to spot Laura's auburn curls through the crowd. "I think I have been ditched."

Landers stretched slightly, peering in the direction Cass was looking. "I don't see...wait. Tall, gorgeous, lovely curls?" At Cass's affirmative nod, Captain Landers snagged one of the bags at Cass's feet with one hand and tugged her along with the other. "I think I spotted her." She led Cass through the crush. "How about that flight? Sorry about that bumpiness at the end, couldn't be helped. Doing all right?"

"Uh, yeah, I guess." Tired and distracted, a bit of Cass's frustration at being left at the gate leaked through.

Glancing at her, Landers smiled. "Hey, I don't think she was deliberately trying to ditch you. It's just that you are, um..."

"Yeah, I know. Short." Cass shrugged. "But still, I hope it's not indicative of the team's attitude toward me. She barely said hi before she took off!" Cass noted that unlike Laura, Landers was at least attempting to shorten her stride to match Cass's.

God, I am exhausted. In the crowd up ahead, she spotted Laura's distinctive hair, turning this way and that, obviously searching for her. *Well, she wouldn't have to search so hard if she had not taken off so fast.*

She watched as Landers tapped Laura on the shoulder to get her attention. "Um, 'scuse me, but I think you lost this." She quirked an eyebrow in Cass's direction. Laura took note of Landers' captain's uniform, then had the good grace to look chagrined as she realized her charge was behind her.

"Uh, yeah." Laura tilted her head at Cass, not meeting her eyes. "Sorry 'bout that. It's crazy in here." She glanced from Cass to the pilot, her gaze lingering on the almost proprietary arm Landers had around Cass's shoulder. "The van is out front. We need to hurry."

Cass turned to Landers and impulsively embraced her. "Thanks so much, for the upgrade and for the rescue." She smiled.

"Not at all." Anne reached into a pocket and pulled out a silver cardholder. She extracted a card and scribbled some information on the back before handing the card to Cass. "My cell and my e-mail, call me if you get lost again." She gave the barest of winks in Laura's direction.

"Got another one of those?" Cass borrowed Landers' pen and scribbled her own information on the back of the woman's own card. "Don't know how the cell stuff works over here, but I'd love it if you could come and see some of the regatta." She paused, then added, "We get some tickets. You know, for family. I'll leave your name at the venues, if you'd like."

The surprise on Landers' face was obvious. "You sure? I mean, those should go to your family." It was only then that she seemed to register that there was nobody at all traveling with Cass. "I'm sorry, I didn't even think. Did you leave someone behind in coach when I bumped you up to first?"

"Oh, no," Cass hastily reassured the pilot. She looked over at Laura, noting that her teammate was checking her watch impatiently. "No, you're good." She bent to pull her bags from the cart, relieved to see that Laura grabbed one too. "I mean it. I'll let them know at the venue. Have them look under my name."

Landers helped Cass lift her backpack up onto her shoulder and then gave her a last, quick hug. "We'll definitely make plans to see you race...and win."

Cass flashed Landers a grateful smile and turned to follow a quickly disappearing Laura out of the concourse. Whatever else happened, she'd at least made one friend here.

CHAPTER SEVEN

The drive from the airport to the Olympic Village, just north of the city, passed in a blur for Cass. It was late afternoon and the streets were just as crowded as the airport had been. Her companion was silent on the drive, muttering occasionally at the scooters and pedestrians who darted in and out of traffic.

So far, her introduction to the team, or one member of it, had not been very positive. Hopefully the other women were more...personable. After two aborted attempts at conversation, Cass gave up and pulled out her camera. The little Canon was her one indulgence in the past year, and she was going to put it to good use. As the van whipped in and out of the endless stream of traffic, Cass snapped what photos she could in the dying light of the day. When the van jerked again to a sudden halt, Cass threw her arm up defensively. "Whoa!"

"Sorry," muttered Laura. "It's nuts out here this time of day."

Wondering if she was warming up slightly, Cass ventured, "I thought they said no cars were allowed in the city for the Games?"

"Not till the actual events begin, and that's not for another six weeks."

Laura didn't take her eyes off the road, nor did she offer any more information, and Cass gave up. At one intersection she watched as a man balanced a pole across his shoulders. From each end of the pole hung suspended two large—and presumably heavy, judging from the bend in the pole—packages. Musicians and vendors competed for attention, and Cass was certain the vendors were winning. One elderly woman in gray, loose-fitting clothing resembling decorative pajamas, held a large, orange bullhorn to her lips and was shouting into it to anyone who came near. Cass assumed she was hoping someone would buy the oranges piled in the cart beside her.

There were bicycles everywhere, two-wheeled and three-wheeled. Cass craned her neck to watch as a three-wheeled version, one wheel in back, two in front, creaked past. On board, in the cargo area up front, was a lime-green refrigerator and a woman. The woman caught Cass's eye and bowed her head in dignified, if silent, greeting as Laura pulled the van past and whipped them around the corner.

It was a blur of color, sound and smell. As they passed one street, Cass saw a large crowd gathering around what looked to be an accident site. The normal volume of the street sounds was ratcheted up here, with men and women waving their arms, punctuating their words with sharp gestures. And over all of it lay the pervasive, stifling humidity.

It was hot.

Suffocatingly hot. Even at, Cass checked her watch, eight fifteen p.m., it was almost too hot to breathe.

Slowly the noise and chaos abated as they neared what was clearly a newer area of the city. Flashes of darkness flew past her window and Cass smelled bursts of green and damp. A park. A large one. More lights and sounds, but this time with a less frenetic feel, and then the van rolled to a stop before a well-lit building resembling an apartment complex.

Cass looked over at Laura, surprised to find her staring straight ahead, her hands gripping the steering wheel so tightly that her knuckles were white. Her features, or what Cass could see of them in the growing darkness and in profile, were set, her expression hard. Cass cleared her throat softly, but no response. Perplexed, she tried again to catch Laura's attention, this time giving a soft cough and reaching out to touch the other woman's arm. Laura's response was far from what she expected.

Laura whipped her head around, her auburn curls flying. She flinched at Cass's touch, then physically recoiled.

Cass opened her mouth to speak but something stopped her. Something in Laura's eyes. For a moment, a long moment, Cass realized that Laura wasn't seeing *her*, Cass, but...something else. Or some*one*. Again, as it had in the airport, came that brief ache as she looked into Laura's sea-green eyes. The pain that swam there...lurked. It tugged at Cass. Again she tried to speak, but this time it was Laura who stopped her. In a flash, that brief window into her teammate was closed. Slammed shut. Instead Cass was met with a steely gaze that very clearly said, "Back off."

Recoiling from the sudden emptiness, Cass could only stutter, "A-are you, okay?"

Laura started again, almost as if she was surprised to see Cass in the van with her. Her face cleared and the lines Cass had seen were replaced by the blank, almost indifferent look she'd worn earlier. "Yes. Fine. Let's get going. I think there's enough light left for me to get out on the water." Slamming the door behind her, Laura headed toward the building, leaving Cass inside the van, her mouth open.

"Uh, fine. Great." Muttering to herself as she grabbed her duffel, Cass continued sarcastically to the empty van, "No, don't bother, I've got it." Now completely alone she continued, "Oh, you're too kind, no really, I can manage." This last was said to Laura's retreating back; the woman clearly had no intention of helping her, or even welcoming her to the squad. *It's gotta be better inside, right?*

Cass checked in with the security at the front desk and

endured the paperwork and identification-check process to get her official credentials. She did stop and stare in wonder at the official plastic-encased identification tag the guard handed her. There it was, in neat black lettering on a white background. "Cassandra Flynn, United States." Just below her name were the five Olympic rings and despite her exhaustion she couldn't resist running her fingers slowly over first her name and then the rings.

The guard cleared his throat and Cass sheepishly ducked her head and shrugged. She glanced up to find him smiling back at her, his eyes sparkling with kindness. Cass thanked him again and reached down for her bag. She hung the badge from her neck and looked around in confusion. Laura was nowhere to be seen. Now dead-on-her-feet tired, she numbly followed the guard's directions to the elevators and prayed she could stay awake long enough to be coherent when she met the remainder of the team.

CHAPTER EIGHT

Cass slept for nearly eight hours. She gradually came awake to the sound of muffled conversation and soft laughter just outside her door. She was stiff, the kind of stiff that came from sleeping in one position for a long time. She rolled onto her back and began to stretch, slowly bringing circulation back to limbs that still felt leaden with fatigue. As she woke she took note of her room, taking in details she'd missed the night before. The ceiling looked closer than she expected and it took her a moment to remember that she was on the top bunk. With a loud sigh she extended her arms and arched her back, a soft groan escaping as she indulged in the stretch. The door to her room opened and a blond head peeked around the corner.

"Hey roomie, you're awake?"

"Um...yeah. Hey, Amy."

Amy Lindquist, coxswain of the eight-member crew, stepped all the way into the room and closed the door. Cass vaguely remembered being reintroduced to her the night—or was it day?—before. Cass's memories of her arrival in the village were hazy, but she had managed to exchange a few words with her roommate before she'd climbed up and into bed. Amy grinned up at her and plopped into a small plastic chair.

"I'm surprised you remember, you were pretty out of it when you got here. Long flight, eh?"

Cass nodded as she sat up and swung her legs over the side of the bunk. With a light grunt she pushed and dropped down onto the floor to continue her stretching. It felt good to be up and moving. Now that she was awake, however, her body was making it known that it had been neglected too long.

"Yeah. Excuse me a sec." Cass ducked into the small bathroom, Amy's voice following her.

"I totally get it. We, the team I mean, we trained in Japan for six weeks before coming here. When we landed there I was really wiped out. But that made the transition to here a lot easier. But man...that flight."

Cass came out, wiping her face and swallowing the last taste of the toothpaste she'd just used. She felt almost human again. Next up on her agenda were food and meeting the team, hopefully in that order.

"So, what's on the schedule for the day? How much have I missed?" She glanced around then asked, "What time is it?"

"It's just after two thirty in the morning."

"Oh." Cass sat on the lower bunk and stared at her roommate. "Wow."

Amy fished in her gym bag and pulled out a Power Bar. She tossed it to Cass, who tore into it eagerly. "Here, this should hold you till morning. You were out. Coach came by after practice but you were already asleep. She told us to let you sleep it out and we'd get you hooked up with the team in the morning."

"Thanks." Cass waved the now empty wrapper at Amy. "How come you're up? I mean, it *is* two thirty in the morning."

Amy grinned again at her, her wide smile prompting Cass to smile in return. "I ah, was out a bit later than I'd planned tonight. My guy's on the men's team and we had a late dinner." Amy grabbed two bottles of water and tossed one to Cass who drank gratefully.

"Thanks, I hate long flights. I always get so thirsty."

"Me too. Coach says to make sure we stay hydrated here."

Cass nodded and stretched again, enjoying the flexibility of well-rested muscles. She extended her left leg and then bent it, aware as always of the increased tension along the scarred skin.

"Mind if I ask?" Amy gestured with her bottle of water to Cass's leg.

"No, I don't mind." Cass took another long swallow of water. "Me versus a pizza guy. I lost." She flexed her leg again, pleased that despite the long flight she had no pain or stiffness.

"Ouch."

"Yup."

Amy studied her for a moment. "That's why you were off the circuit last year."

"Yeah. Long recovery." Cass finished her bottle and looked for the trash, wondering how she could gracefully change the subject. She didn't want to focus on her leg anymore. She'd wasted enough time, *lost* enough time to a stupid accident. Now she just wanted to move forward. "So, I guess tomorrow—"

The door to their room opened and a new face peeked in. She glanced from Amy to Cass and back again then turned and spoke to someone outside.

"Hey, yeah, they're up," she called. She poked her face back inside. "Mind if we come in?" She addressed her comment to Amy and Cass as she stepped inside, followed by three other women wearing USA team shorts and T's.

"No, come on in. Cass, this is Sarah Sullivan, your doubles partner. These three are Kim, Ellie and Jan. They're numbers four, five and seven on the eight-boat." Amy pointed to each woman in turn as she identified their positions on the long eight-woman boat.

As opposed to Cass and her new team partner, Sarah, the rowers on the eight-boat each used a single oar. The odd-numbered rowers rowed the starboard, or right-hand, side and the evens rowed the port side. Cass studied the newcomers appraisingly, just as they did her. Kim and Ellie epitomized the physique of rowers placed in the center of the boat; solid, well-muscled, broad-shouldered and probably very strong. Jan, too, matched Cass's ideal of a Seven. She was tall, lithe and obviously fit, and she radiated a calm that made Cass feel completely at ease.

Cass rose to shake the newcomers' hands. She finished with Sarah, saying, "I remember you. Nationals, two years ago?" At Sarah's nod Cass continued, "Your boat beat mine by a hair."

Sarah laughed. "Yep, I remember. It was pretty close." She angled her head, reminding Cass of a curious terrier. "You didn't stay for the after-party. I remember our coach wanting to talk to you."

"I couldn't, I was due back in Wisconsin to start my clinical rotation the next morning. My schedule was pretty tight. I almost didn't make that last heat."

"Too bad, we had a lot of fun."

The four newcomers settled on the floor in various poses. Sarah grabbed a pillow from Amy's bunk and bunched it up under her head as she stretched out on the floor.

"Hey. I have to sleep on that, you know," protested Amy.

"Oh, lighten up, Ames. The floor's clean." She grinned up at Cass. "When's your family getting here?"

Struggling to keep her voice light, Cass shook her head. "They're ah...no. Not coming."

"Nobody?" Ellie sat forward, exchanging glances with Jan.

"N-no." Cass forced a fake yawn, hoping to deflect anymore questions. There wasn't a chance in hell her "family" would make any effort at all to be here.

Jan, perhaps sensing Cass's discomfort, filled the suddenly awkward silence. "So Cass, you're going to bring us some new mojo, right?"

"Sorry?"

"Mojo. New. We need it."

"Oh. Yeah. I was sorry to hear of Pam's injury, will she be all right?" Cass knew from gossip around the docks back in San Diego that Sarah's regular doubles partner, Pam Collins, had broken her arm four days after the team transitioned from Japan.

Cass owed her sudden position on the team to a series of injuries, first to Pam and then to the reserve rower, Gail Kennedy.

Sarah nodded. "Yeah, she should be okay. I wanted her to fly back to the States to get it checked out right away, but she didn't want to miss the Games."

Cass was surprised. "She's still here?"

"Yeah."

"I look forward to meeting her." Cass smiled shyly at the women sitting around her, glad they'd gotten off the topic of her family. "And I know what you mean about not wanting to miss this."

"Oh, yeah. And you haven't even seen the whole village yet," Ellie chimed in. She tapped Cass's leg in a friendly manner. "You're not just here because Gail was stupid."

"C'mon, El, that's not fair," Jan protested, but the others waved her objection away.

"You know it's true." Sarah's voice was curt, she was obviously still angry about the reserve rower's injury.

"I don't understand. What happened?" Cass looked from one woman to the other, then finally to Amy for an explanation. The little coxswain shrugged.

"Gail Kennedy. You know, the reserve? We had a day off last week, and she decided to go exploring some of the rock formations north of the city. She freaking fell and tore a muscle in her shoulder. Shit, Sheila was furious. Still is, I think."

Amy's explanation cleared up some confusion for Cass. She'd wondered why the team wasn't using the reserve doubles rower and now she knew.

Kim slid down the wall and pushed her feet into Jan's leg. "We don't have to get into this again, folks. It's late." She gave Cass a gentle smile. "We just wanted to say 'hey' and welcome you to the team." She glanced at the others before adding, "Laura looked to be on a tear when she got back last night. She went straight to the gym."

The others chuckled, apparently the capriciousness of the stroke of the eight crew was well known to them. Cass thought again of the abrupt welcome she'd gotten yesterday and wondered what had prompted it. She also remembered the brief flash of pain she'd seen on Laura's face in the van just as they'd arrived in the village. "I thought she was mad at me for some reason."

Sarah shook her head as she stood and tossed Amy's pillow back onto the bed. "No worries, it wasn't you. Laura can be a bit...intense."

Ellie snorted as she hauled Kim and Jan up with her and headed toward the door. "Intense. Yeah, that's a good word for it."

"C'mon, guys," Jan spoke up. "Give her a break." She looked to where Cass was sitting and shrugged. "You know how it is. Girl's gotta have a bit of an attitude to be a really good stroke. Laura's–"

"*Really* good at what she does," Ellie finished with a laugh.

"Say what you will, the woman's a hell of a stroke and you know it." Amy yawned and waved the other women out. "G'wan, I'm beat. The welcoming committee's done its job."

Sarah turned back and smiled again at Cass. "Welcome to the team, Cass. I'm looking forward to our practices."

She closed the door behind her, leaving Cass and Amy alone once again. Cass rose and waited for Amy to return from the bathroom. Then she flipped off the light and climbed back up to her bunk. Her first meeting with her new teammates had gone pretty well, she thought. She stretched again and, after a whispered good night to Amy, slipped in to sleep again.

Amy listened as Cass resettled herself above her, considering what she'd learned about the team's newest member, and what she'd seen last evening when Laura had returned with Cass from the airport.

She'd known Laura for more than four years, since the two had rowed at Cal as freshmen. It had been Laura who'd gotten Amy involved with the sport, Laura who'd convinced her that she'd make a good cox for the team. The two progressed together from JV to varsity, and together had led Cal to some spectacular victories. Amy knew Laura inside and out, and it was easy to see that something had upset her friend, something beyond being pushed out of the gym for one afternoon.

The bed above her creaked as Cass shifted, and Amy reviewed what she knew of Cass. The e-mail she had gotten last night from a friend back at the training center in San Diego had not been much help. Jackie had described Cass as a bit of a loner, someone who did not socialize much with the rest of the group. *Of course,* Amy mused, *Jackie's mad as hell* she *wasn't selected to fill Gail's slot.* What Jackie had not said was as interesting as what she had. Amy did not remember a single thing in her e-mail that mentioned Cass's course times or her abilities. Amy shrugged at the lack, still irritated with both her teammate's lack of judgment and the injury that forced Coach to pull Gail from the regatta.

Amy sighed and rolled onto her side, punching her pillow into submission. Her eyes drifted closed as she thought again of Coach's decisions. Pam's broken arm had been first, and Amy knew Coach had had no choice but to replace her. But Gail's injury was less severe, and Amy was fairly certain she'd have been good enough to get their double's boat through to a decent finish, although probably not a medal. Coach's reaction, however, had been a surprise. Sheila had been furious with Gail for deciding to go rock climbing on a team rest day.

Whatever else she might have thought about Laura, the team's injuries, or the coach's decision were lost as Amy surrendered to sleep, content to at least have a full squad once again.

CHAPTER NINE

"Look, this isn't working."

The disgust in Sarah's voice grated on Cass's last nerve, and she bit her tongue to keep from snapping back. The trouble was that Cass, too, knew something was off; something had *been* off since they'd put in to the water earlier today. It seemed the harder Cass worked to fit her style with Sarah's, the worse their performance got. She groaned and collapsed backward, letting her momentum slide the seat until her head rested against the splash guard. She kicked her feet free of the shoes bolted into the stretcher, toed off her socks and let her feet dangle over each side of the slim craft into the water below. The coolness was a shock to her overheated system and she could see steam rising off her stomach as she tried to catch her breath. Years of training kept her hands on the oars, and she absently pushed her arms against the soft current, gently holding the shell in position. Before her, equally tired and apparently just as frustrated, Sarah Sullivan sat bent over her own oars, her back rising and falling with each deep breath.

"I know it's not working, but I don't know what the hell the problem is," Cass gasped out between breaths. The air felt... *thicker* here. *Almost chewable*, she thought.

"It's not as if you're not trying hard enough. Shit, you work harder than the rooks." Sarah, too, was blowing hard from their last workout.

"What's going wrong then?"

"Damned if I know." Sarah shook her head and slipped off her red USA Rowing hat. She ran her hands through her short blond hair, pushing it up on end. She reminded Cass of a rooster, all fire and energy and now, with her hair poking out at odd angles, it was enough to make Cass giggle.

"What's so funny?"

"Nothing. Just tired, I think." This was their fourth run of the day and Cass was at her limit. The first run had been their first time together on the water, just an easy row down the course to get each other's rhythm. The second run had been for time and for Coach to record it on video to see where they needed work. The run time hadn't been too bad, but it was nowhere near the level they'd need to medal six weeks from now. The last two times down the course, Cass felt they had just gotten steadily worse.

As the stroke, the rower closest to the back end of the boat—the end farthest from the finish—it was Cass who called the stroke rate and it fell to her to decide when they made their sprint for the finish, when they stepped up their rate. Except, for some reason, that wasn't working for them. When Cass had rowed bow, with Sarah calling the rowing rate, their speed had been better, but their timing off. When they'd switched back, as they had for the latest run, the speed was down but the timing better. Cass pushed herself up and waited as the coach's launch idled closer, its throaty engine coughing as it, too, fought the current. Cass squinted against the sun and sat up a bit straighter when she noticed that Laura was piloting the shallow-hulled boat.

Laura was silhouetted against the late afternoon sunlight, her auburn hair pulled into a ponytail and threaded through the back of her team cap. A faded Cal-Berkeley T-shirt stretched across her shoulders and chest, and her long, tanned legs disappeared into worn shorts. Cass caught her breath, surprised again at the tingle that ran through her as she watched Laura deftly maneuver the boat alongside their fragile scull. It was the same brief feeling she'd gotten at the airport three days earlier. As Laura cut back the throttle and checked their position, her eyes caught Cass's. They held for a moment, and Cass thought she saw some of her own frustration mirrored there. Cass shrugged ruefully, letting her disappointment over the latest practice run show through. Laura's response was a brief nod in return, her eyes, shadowed by the brim of her hat, gave nothing away. Her expression was... still.

Sarah lifted an oar up toward Coach Sheila, who caught it and braced herself, using the oar as a bridge between the launch and the shell. Sarah asked the coach, "What do you think?"

"I think it's time to come in and review some tape. Something's off and we have to get it fixed." Sheila frowned and rubbed her forehead. "It's frustrating to watch, you're almost there, but..."

"Damn...I know. Cass says so too. We've tried—"

"Flynn needs to sit stern." Laura's voice cut through Sarah's, brusquely interrupting her.

Cass sat forward, frowning at Laura's abrupt tone. She hated being referred to as simply "Flynn," as if she weren't a person. "We've tried that and it—"

"Not this way." At Sheila's nod, Laura continued. "Switch it up. There's no rule that says stern has to call stroke, it's just tradition. Put Flynn in the stern, but Sarah, you call the rate." She paused and addressed Cass for the first time, her tone dismissive. Her head tipped forward just enough so the sun illuminated her face and her cool green gaze ran the length of Cass's injured leg. "Can your leg stand another run at half-speed?"

Cass bristled at Laura's tone and the implication. *She's stunning, but she's a bitch,* flashed through Cass's mind as she jerked upright. Flipping her legs back into the scull, she slid her socks on and her feet back into the shoes. She used the moment to control her temper, but her hands trembled slightly, giving away her anger. *I will not pop off. She's a bitch, but I don't have to row with her. "Can your leg handle it?" Fuck you. My leg is great. It's not beautiful, but it works perfectly. Better than perfect.* She took a deep breath and glared at Laura. "My name is 'Cass,' not 'Flynn,' and my *leg* is fine, thanks." She jerked her head toward Sarah. "We can do another run, full speed, if you want. I'm good to go."

"Fine, whatever." Laura looked again to the coach. "Do you want to do one more run, but with the different setup?"

Cass watched as the coach looked from her to Laura and then over to Sarah, who was staring at Laura with a puzzled expression. With a last glance at Laura and a shrug in Sarah's direction, the coach shook her head. "I think we're done for the day." Sheila raised her hand against Cass's protest. "I know you're eager to get it together, but we have six weeks yet. We don't need to burn it all on day one." She gently pushed Sarah's oar away, sending the small scull drifting back. "Meet you on the dock."

Cass fumed as they slowly rowed back to the magnificent dock the Chinese had built for these Games. The first time she'd seen the facility, she'd felt soothed, almost relaxed. The building seemed to flow with the river, to be a part of it. It blended into its surroundings, almost embraced by the natural bend at the end of the course. Cass had loved it at first sight. The softly curving roof had settled her, calmed her. But not now.

"What the hell is *with* her?"

"You mean Laura?"

"Yeah." Cass's strokes were choppy, reflecting her anger and frustration. "Is she an assistant or something?"

"No. Well, sort of. She wants to coach and really, normally, she's good. Really good. She's the stroke for the eight and Coach relies on her a lot. The assistants are at the gym with the rookies today, and when they're tied up, Coach uses Laura. Don't know what's gotten into her, she's usually not so...well, rude." Sarah looked over her shoulder at Cass. "She's not that bad, really. I've known her for, oh, I dunno, maybe ten months or so. Since the Head of the Charles regatta. She's okay, really."

"I just..." Cass frowned, frustrated. She concentrated on their position in the water for a moment, making sure they were clear of other teams heading in and out of the landing area. "She gets to me, you know? She pretty much ditched me at the airport and hasn't said two polite words to me since."

"She can be a bit...rough is I guess the best way to say it." Sarah shrugged. "She's good though, and that's what counts, right?"

"Yeah, I guess that's what matters." Cass pushed her reaction to Laura's brusque treatment aside, realizing that fatigue was probably making her overreact. She glanced over her shoulder at the approaching dock. "Easy oar," she said, a signal to Sarah to give a lighter stroke as they neared the floating structure and allow the small craft to continue its forward momentum. Checking her distance again, Cass called, "Drop," and let her oars rest in the water, slowing the boat. As the bow of the boat passed the dock, she continued, "Bow out." In time with her words, she flipped open the oar gate and lifted her dockside oar out of the water. She lifted it high, making sure the blade was well clear of the pilings.

"Stern out." Sarah followed suit.

"Lean away." Both women leaned away from the dock, allowing their dockside oars to hover above it as they floated in. They walked their hands down the teakwood dock planks and slowly brought the stern of the boat around so the scull was parallel to the dock. Cass remained in the boat and held it steady while Sarah climbed out, flipping her waterside oar gates open as she stepped onto the floating surface. Cass handed the oars to her and both women quickly and efficiently went through the motions of getting the scull ready to lift out of the water. Jenny Paulson, one of the team's designated riggers, ran down the dock to help.

"Jenn, you help me get the boat out. Cass, you can grab the oars, okay?"

"I can do it, you know. There's nothing wrong with me." Cass's sharp reply clearly startled Jenny and Sarah, and both women stared at her in silence. Jenny glanced quickly between the two women, then silently began wiping down the oars, keeping well clear of the other two.

"What the hell was that about?" Sarah stepped close to Cass, her usually friendly face suffused with red, her eyes tense and angry.

"It's my job to get the boat out of the water with you, not hers." Cass was still smarting from Laura's question about her leg. Her damned leg. What made it worse was the knowledge that if Coach had asked for that last run down the course, Cass wasn't one hundred percent certain she could have done it, despite saying that she could. That knowledge, added to Laura's tone, pushed Cass over the edge.

"I know it's your job. It's my job too. I'm tired, you're tired. I figured if we had someone here who wasn't, she could do some of the lifting." Sarah backed up a step, staring at Cass. She glanced quickly down at Cass's scarred leg and back up again. "You think it's because you were hurt before? Because of what Laura said earlier?"

"Well, I—"

"Oh, for Pete's sake! Laura pissed you off and you're mad at *me*?" Sarah shook her head. "Nice, Cass. Fine. Jenny, you and superwoman here can lift the damned boat out of the water and *I'll* take the oars in." Sarah held out her hand for Jenny's towel, her movements jerky and tense.

Jenny moved to the edge of the dock nearest the stern, resting her hands on her knees, waiting for Cass to give the command to lift the boat.

Cass scrubbed her face with her hands, frustrated with herself. *Shit. Shitshitshitshit. Fix this, Cass, and right now.* She stepped forward, her hand halfway to Sarah's shoulder before she let it drop to her side. "Sarah. Stop."

Sarah turned, her eyes still angry, her freckles standing out on her sunburned face. She said nothing, simply stood waiting for Cass to continue.

"I'm sorry." Cass slid her team cap off her head, letting her hair fall out of its holder and onto her shoulders. She scratched her head, relieving the itch that always started when she took off her hat. She was stalling and she knew it. "I'm sorry, really. I guess I'm..." She shrugged. "I am a bit sensitive about the leg and yeah, I let Laura get to me just now." Hat back on her head, she lifted her gaze from the dock to Sarah's face. "You haven't asked, nobody has. I appreciate that. It took me a long time to get back into shape and I'm there, but sometimes..." She shrugged. "I get tired of feeling like I have to prove something, you know?"

"What the hell could you have to prove, Cass? You're here, in Beijing, getting ready for the Olympics!" Sarah shook her head, her blond ponytail whipping back and forth. "Jeez Cass, give yourself a bit of a break, okay? And maybe some of the rest of us, too."

Cass nodded, hoping she'd made it okay for both of them.

Sarah leaned on the oars for a moment, her expression thoughtful. Cass had opened the topic and if there was any hope of them doing well as a team they had to trust each other. "Will you tell me about it? Sometime?"

"I don't know if I...I don't like to talk about it, really."

"Will you at least tell me if it gives you trouble? I need to know Cass, just like you need to know when I'm tired, or hurting. We're a team. Okay?"

Nodding slowly, Cass kept her eyes on Sarah's. There was no judgment there, no pity. Only concern. *It's not always about you, Cass.* "Yeah, okay, I get it." She shifted, her back and legs sore from their workout. "So, in the interest of teamwork, I'm going to confess. I hurt like hell. Can we go back to your original idea?"

"Sure." A smile lit Sarah's face and she poked Cass in the shoulder. "That wasn't so hard, was it?" Sarah chuckled as Cass grimaced and moved aside. Together she and Jenny emptied the shell of the water bottles and sweatshirts she and Cass had used during their training runs.

Cass stepped aside with the oars, automatically checking the edges of the blades to be sure they hadn't been damaged during their use today. She grabbed the towel Jenny tossed her way and finished the job of wiping down the sixteen-foot shafts and blades. The dock rocked slightly as Sarah and Jenny lifted the light scull out of the water and up over their heads, Sarah's commands audible only to the three of them. Cass caught Sarah's Gatorade bottle as it dropped out of the overturned craft, stuffing it into the bag she had left on the dock earlier.

Cass turned as the sound of the coach's launch puttering

through the soft current as it drew near the permanent dock farther down the shore caught her attention. She stopped, the sixteen-foot oars balanced on her shoulders, and rested against the dock piling as she watched Laura maneuver the boat into position. Great stroke or not, Laura had a chip on her shoulder and apparently a large one where Cass was concerned. *Whatever's eating her is not my problem. Focus on what you came here to do.* She glanced again at Laura as the team's captain secured the launch. The setting sun, already tinged orange by the thickness of the Beijing air, burnished Laura's hair to an enticing, fire-lit auburn and highlighted her tanned physique. The view was...mouth-watering, if you didn't have to think of the personality that went with the body. *Too bad.* With a small sigh, Cass shifted the oars slightly and, tightening her grip on her and Sarah's bags, strode up the dock toward the boathouse.

CHAPTER TEN

"So, you're the gal who's gonna help my little girl's boat win, eh?" John Sullivan grinned as he shook Cass's hand. His grip was as solid as he was, his fingers warm and dry as they enveloped Cass's. He squeezed once, gently, then let go to wrap his arm around Sarah.

"I'll do my best, sir," Cass answered with a smile.

"Oh, Dad. Cut it out." Sarah nudged her dad's shoulder as she reached out and pulled her partner Pam over. "You're gonna make Pam feel bad."

John immediately moved around Sarah to wrap Pam in a gentle but sincere hug. "C'mon, Sarah, our Pammie knows I love her to bits. Bad luck, this injury." He kept one arm around Pam as he pulled Sarah back to his side. "Couldn't be prouder of my two girls here."

Cass laughed along with the rest as John steered the large party into the restaurant. He'd swept into the village yesterday, the unspoken leader of the group of parents and family who had traveled to Beijing to support the team. Within hours of his arrival, big John Sullivan had organized a "team and family" dinner at a nearby restaurant and declared the next night a night off for all and sundry. Cass could see where Sarah got the sparkle in her eyes, though she was certain her teammate's calm demeanor came from her mother. Carol Sullivan was quiet where her husband was loud. She'd come in, quietly following in his wake, and introduced herself, then promptly taken over the organizing duties. She was also, Cass discovered, a hard woman to say no to.

Cass's first instinct had been to decline the Sullivans' invitation, not wanting to intrude on any family time. She'd quickly learned, however, that to John Sullivan, "family" was a term for which he had his own definition. Cass followed the long line of her teammates through the large restaurant and into the back room John had reserved. Carol Sullivan was waving for them to sit where they wished, and Cass watched, wanting to be careful not to sit between family members. She didn't have any family coming to the Games and she wanted to be sure her teammates got to sit with their loved ones. When the dust settled, she found herself at the far end of a long table. She took one of the last empty seats and settled in, leaning over to hear what Jan, the number seven rower of the long boat, was saying. The noise was too great, and she just waved Jan off with a smile and instead concentrated on her menu.

"Ah, sorry. Are you saving this?"

Cass looked up to find Laura standing uncertainly behind the only remaining empty chair in the room. She hadn't seen Laura since their encounter on the water yesterday afternoon, and Cass flashed back suddenly to the embarrassment and anger she'd felt when Laura had eyed her injured leg. She felt her temper rise before she clamped down firmly. Now wasn't the time or place and she struggled to rein in her feelings. *Of course the only empty seat in the room is next to me*, she seethed.

Something of what she was feeling must have shown on her

face, because Laura took a step back and looked around the room for another place. "Never mind, I'll—"

"No." Cass reached out and pulled the empty chair back in invitation. "No. I'm sorry. Sit here."

"If you're saving it—"

"I'm not." It wouldn't kill her to have Laura sit next to her; it wasn't like she had to make conversation with the woman, after all. Cass turned back to Jan only to find Jan still engrossed in conversation with her brothers about the events they planned to see. She opened up her menu to distract herself and realized that everything was printed in, as was to be expected, Chinese. Cass sighed. She glanced at Laura out of the corner of her eye and saw that Laura, too, was sitting and staring uncomprehendingly down at her menu. Not talking with anyone else, not even really listening to the surrounding chatter. Just staring down. Cass sighed again. This was ridiculous.

"Hey, Laura," Cass began, determined to make an effort. "I, ah, wanted to say thanks for picking me up at the airport last week." She shrugged. "I know it's a bit late, but—"

"No problem. Coach asked me to." Laura's tone was dismissive.

The silence grew between them and Cass found herself determined to break it. She was getting nothing but "leave me alone" vibes from this woman, but something in her just wouldn't let it be. She gestured toward the menu. "Got any ideas?"

Laura barely looked up at her. "For what?"

It was like pulling teeth. "Dinner." Cass wiggled the menu. "Unless you can read Chinese, I'm stumped as to what to order."

Before Laura could speak, John Sullivan stood up. "Ladies and gentlemen, can I have your attention for just a moment?" He waited for the general hubbub to die down. "I just wanted to thank you all for coming out tonight. I know we're a big crowd in this small room, but we're also a big family, and I wanted to start us all off right." He looked around the room again, his gaze resting for a moment on Sarah and Pam, then on his wife, and finally on Cass. "We've got some new members of the family to welcome, so don't be shy and make sure you say hello if you don't know someone." He gave Cass the barest of winks. "I know some of you have family still coming in, so I was thinking we might squeeze in one more of these shindigs just before the regatta, if we can get Coach, here, to agree. Whaddya say?"

Everyone applauded and Sheila stood up to shake John's hand. "Who can say no to Big John, eh?" she asked the room with a forbearing grin.

"Terrific!" John raised his glass high and offered a brief toast. "To the U.S. Women's Squad. Tear 'em up, girls!"

A chorus of "Hear, hear!" followed his salute and Cass took a long drink of her ice water, appreciating the cold as it washed down her dry throat.

John waved for attention again, lifting his menu high. "I know this menu is hard to read, so I have some help for us."

At his signal a tall man stepped up beside him and began to explain, by number, each item on the menu, making Cass's decision for dinner much easier. She leaned back in her chair with a sigh of relief, her shoulder accidentally brushing Laura's. "Oh, sorry."

Laura's voice was pitched low to cut through the noise in the room. "Not a problem." She paused for a long moment and then offered, "Look, I want to apologize for yesterday."

"Why?"

"Why? Because...well, I was rude."

Cass tipped her head. "Yeah, you were, but...well, don't take this the wrong way, but you don't strike me as the type to realize that."

Laura's tiny smile was so small that Cass almost missed it. "I had some help."

"Oh."

"Anyway," Laura turned to face Cass. "I just wanted to say I'm sorry if I hurt your feelings."

Cass studied the woman seated next to her. Laura was, for the first time, attempting a civil conversation. As she met Laura's eyes, she felt again that same frission of excitement that she'd felt at the airport and again on the water before... well, before Laura had spoken. She wondered if Laura felt it too. Cass finally nodded. "Thanks, I appreciate it. I...well, I was probably a bit hypersensitive, too, so…" She shrugged. "No hard feelings."

Laura didn't respond, but she didn't entirely shut Cass out either. She turned back to her menu and Cass felt there was less tension between them. It wasn't much, but it was a start. Suddenly Cass was glad that the only empty seat available had been next to hers.

CHAPTER ELEVEN

"Watch that leg extension, Crosby. You don't want to push that knee too hard. We have another week before the heats begin."

Coach Sheila made her way around the gym, speaking to each woman working her sets on the machines. Coming upon Amy, Sheila smiled. Amy did not row, she called the rate of speed and kept the boat on track and in line, all crucial to the success of the crew. Despite not being a rower on her team, Amy could be found wherever the team was, and right now she was spotting Cass as Cass lifted weights. Sheila was glad to see Amy had taken Cass under her wing; she had known pairing them up as roommates would be a good idea. Coming into an established team was hard enough; coming into one just six weeks before the Olympics was darned near impossible.

So far, Cass's maturity had been a benefit; she'd navigated the tricky "getting to know you" waters well enough, especially considering her rocky start with Laura. The other members of the squad had taken to Cass readily enough, especially after watching her determined effort to mesh with her doubles partner. Sarah in particular had warmly welcomed Cass, taking her skill and competence as a sign that her own run of bad luck had changed.

Sheila had been worried about how Sarah would adapt to rowing with someone new. The injured doubles team member, Pam, was not only Sarah's rowing partner, but her girlfriend. It took time to build a rapport between two rowers, to know each other's rhythms. Six weeks wasn't enough time by anyone's stretch of imagination to build a dynamic and functioning team. Sheila watched as Cass changed weight sets, and opened her mouth to comment, only to stop when she saw Sarah reach over, making an adjustment to Cass's hand position. As she made a note on her clipboard, Sheila thought again of the injury that had brought Cass to the team. Gail Kennedy's fall on the team's off day and subsequent rock climbing related muscle tear had killed her boat's chances at a medal, and more importantly to the coach, had shown Sheila that Gail was not committed to the team's success. Cass, Sheila realized, was an entirely different story. No, she needn't have worried. Sarah and Cass were blending their styles well and beginning to anticipate each other's moves. Three weeks of intense, focused practice together had smoothed out their rough edges, once again giving Sheila hope of the doubles team performing credibly at this regatta.

Sheila watched Cass finish her set and then set up to spot Amy, Sarah at her side watching them both. Seeing Cass's eyes follow another rower as she made her way across the room Sheila followed Cass's gaze and spotted Laura adjusting the settings of the gym's stationary bike. Truth be told, it was Laura who'd found the key to making the combination of Sarah and Cass work. With Laura as the stroke for the eight and captain of the squad, Sheila relied a great deal on her, and she had not let her down. She worked incredibly hard, was focused and was in top shape.

As if she knew Sheila was thinking of her, Laura glanced up and caught her eye. She gave the coach a brief nod and, barely sparing a glance around the gym for the rest of her team, continued her solo workout.

Of course she's working out alone...I don't think I've ever seen her spend one-on-one time with anyone.

Sheila knew Laura's story; any coach worth her salt knew what made her athletes tick...or not. While she appreciated the work and results she got from Laura's dedication, it would be nice to see her lose a little of her intense focus once in a while. Glancing back at the look on Cass's face as she distractedly listened to Amy's chatter, Sheila paused. She again followed the line of Cass's gaze and saw the newest squad member's focus completely on her most reticent team member. Stepping backward, she lifted her clipboard and made a few more notes, all the while watching the one-sided communication before her. Finally, she handed her instructions to an assistant and left the gym, wondering if Cass Flynn might not be just what Laura needed to move on.

CHAPTER TWELVE

"Hey, shove over, will you?"

Cass nodded and slid deeper into the booth as Sarah waved her girlfriend Pam onto the padded bench then squeezed in next to her. Cass shifted over, careful not to jar Pam's arm where it rested in its sling. Across from them, Amy, Kim and Ellie crowded into the booth, leaving Jan to pull a chair up to the end of the table, waving over the waitress as she did so.

"Anyone mind if I order for us?"

A chorus of no's followed and Jan ordered drinks for everyone with an aplomb Cass envied. She glanced around the booth, a bit surprised to find herself crowded into a strange restaurant with newfound friends. When Amy had pulled her out of the gym, she had expected it would be just the two of them touring the city. To her surprise several of the women from the eight had joined them, and Cass found herself part of an excited, chattering group of women. Shifting again to give more room to the others, she considered again how she fit with the group. She'd never been the one in the booth with a gang, she'd always either been the waitress or the person walking past the window. On the outside looking in. Being a part of the group inside was a new thing. A good thing.

"So," said Jan after the waitress left them. "What's next for us?"

"Amy's in charge." Kim slid the bowl of fried noodles closer and began to munch.

"Me? Who made me the tour guide?"

"Oh, come on, Ames. You've been in charge of this little party since this morning. So," she echoed Jan. "What's next?"

"Don't know. Depends on what Jan's ordered us for food."

"Oh, you wait and see." Jan reached down the table and pulled the fried noodles back in front of her. She looked over toward Cass who'd said nothing yet and was simply watching. "So, Cass, what's your story?"

"Story?"

Sarah leaned back in the booth, her arm around Pam as they nestled together. "Cass's story is that she's brilliant and is saving our butts."

"Amen," echoed Pam with a rueful smile at her partner before turning to nudge Cass. "Seriously, Cass. I'm glad you're here. If I can't row with Sarah, I'm glad it's you."

Cass was saved from having to answer by the waitress's return, arms laden with steaming bowls of rice and plates of delicious, colorful foods. Amy and Kim began doling out portions as the others claimed various dishes, leaving Cass to ponder Pam's words. She'd been nervous about meeting Pam, since she was essentially taking the other woman's place on the team, but each time they'd had a chance to talk, Pam had been nothing but warm and welcoming to her.

As everyone settled down to her food, Cass took a moment to sort out her answer to Jan's original question. She knew it was bound to come up again.

What *was* her story, really? Boring, certainly.

With dinner came small cups of sweet-smelling liquid that burned on the first swallow but then became increasingly more appealing. Cass relaxed and laughed more as dinner continued, joining in the gentle ribbing of Amy and her appetite as plates were passed around a second time. It was hard for her to slip out of her usual role of observer and to just let herself relax and be a part of things. The drink, which Jan told them was rice wine, helped. Soon she found herself cracking up at another of Ellie's bad puns and joining in as the others egged Amy on in her quest to try the spiciest dish the restaurant had to offer.

As dinner wound down, the question, as Cass had known it would, came around again. Kim nudged Cass's newly refilled cup of rice wine toward her and said, "Hey, wait, let's get back to the important stuff. Cass, I think it's your turn. You don't have anyone coming out here for you?"

Cass, quite comfortably numb by this point, just shrugged. "Nope."

"What's the deal with that?"

Shrugging, Cass worked to keep her voice level as she answered. "No deal, just...no family, really."

Amy, perhaps sensing Cass's discomfort, spoke up. "It's not like Cass is the only one with nobody coming. It would have cost my brother a ton to get his ticket, and he would have had to leave his girl at home."

"True," said Ellie. "My folks barely managed it."

"Still," Jan probed. "Cass, nobody back home pining?"

Cass looked closely at Jan, wondering what was behind the question. She studied her, seeing nothing but curiosity in Jan's gaze. Glancing around the table, she could see the others waiting for her answer. Again, she could sense nothing but genuine friendly curiosity. "Nope. I...well, I guess I've just never, you know. Been in love."

"Who's talking about love?" Amy slammed her glass down on the table, sloshing the last of her drink in her enthusiasm. "We're talkin' wild, hot, monkey-sex."

The women around the table erupted in laughter, taking the focus off Cass and she was grateful. Sarah began teasing Amy about her many purported conquests and Ellie and Kim joined in.

Shifting uncomfortably, Cass wished there was a way she could slide out of the booth before they remembered that she hadn't answered. Unfortunately, she was tucked between Pam and the window. She sighed.

Pam nudged Cass's shoulder. "Are we making you uncomfortable? We all sort of did this when we made the team, back in San Diego. I think Jan and Ellie...well, they're protective of Laura, and—"

"Laura?" Cass kept her voice as low as Pam's, glad the others' attention was elsewhere. "I don't understand. Why would they—"

"Hey! After this let's go check out the Bird's Nest!" Amy pulled out her map and began muttering furiously over it, Ellie and Jan leaning in to help her.

Smiling, Pam leaned back into Sarah's arm and shrugged, answering Cass's question. "I don't know. I just know that you're getting the third degree in a more, um, concentrated form than we all got a couple of months ago. Don't worry about it."

Cass nodded and reached for the bottle of wine in the middle of the table. She never drank much, but tonight she felt the need.

CHAPTER THIRTEEN

Cass pushed open the door to the common room assigned to the U.S. team and grandly waved her teammates inside. Laura looked up from her book as the laughing women burst through the doors. Their breathless laughter was apparently contagious and a small half smile crept across Laura's features, and she raised an eyebrow as the team joined her.

Cass, Amy, Sarah and several others on the team had been sightseeing in the city all afternoon. The goal, according to Amy, had been to "get as used to the pea-soup air as possible." Laura had decided not to join them, telling Amy that she preferred to stay and watch some of the other squads practice their runs down the course. Amy had tried hard to persuade Laura to come and had been a bit miffed that she'd declined. Apparently over her anger, the tiny coxswain bounced across the room and leaned over the arm of the chair in which Laura was curled.

"What'cha reading, Laura-dora?"

A second eyebrow joined the first and Laura leaned her head back to focus on Amy's too-close face. "Laura-dora? What the heck is that?"

"It's your new mickmane, er, nickname." The women with Amy snickered and settled themselves on the couches and chairs around the conversation pit.

"Ames? Have you been into the sake?"

"Nope."

"No?"

"Nope-a-rooney." More snickers followed as Amy slowly slid her small frame over the arm of the chair and into Laura's lap. Laura's eyebrows rose higher and she bit back a smile. Sober Amy was hard to resist, her infectious enthusiasm making her a fun companion. Inebriated Amy was hysterical.

"So...to what do I owe the pleasure of your...non-saked up company?"

"Rice."

By now the rest of the women were laughing out loud; Sarah was wiping tears from her face, her arm around her girlfriend who also convulsed with mirth. They were slumped together on the low couch. Sitting on the floor, her back propped up against their knees, was Cass, trying to focus on the women before her. Others were sprawled in various positions of comfort around the common room, enjoying the show. Cass caught her breath as Laura looked around at the laughing bunch, her gaze resting briefly on Cass's as she tried again to make sense of Amy's words. Oh, those green eyes.

"Rice?"

"Uh-huh. Rice swine. Drunken piggies." That sent the women howling to the floor, and Cass could see that Laura was no closer to the answer to why her boat's cox was apparently drunk as a frat boy on a Saturday night. Laura gently shifted Amy off her lap and onto the floor.

"Cass? Care to share how a pig could get your roommate drunk?"

Cass, still chuckling and wiping her eyes, tried to catch her breath. She could see the light of humor in Laura's eyes, the hint of suppressed laughter in her tone. It was the first time she'd seen the stoic woman smile—or almost smile. "Not a pig, wine. You know, rice wine? Well, we had some with lunch, which was pork and one thing led to another and..."

"Ah. Rice-swine." Laura chuckled softly, watching as Amy carefully tried to focus on her fingertips. "Um, Amy? I think we ought to get you into bed."

"Oh, Laura, I thought you'd never ask." Amy's overly dramatic and slightly breathless reply sent the group into gales of laughter again, except for Cass.

Amy's words struck her and she sat, frozen on the pillows on the floor. *Ow. Damn. Well, that was a surprise. I guess Laura and Amy...what do you care? The woman pisses you off, remember?* Still, Cass was surprised by how much Amy's response to Laura's innocent words twisted her guts. *Get a grip, pal. We've barely said ten words to each other and most of them not very warm. Amy and Laura. Damn.*

Suddenly sober, Cass shoved herself up from the floor. She turned her back on Laura as she easily lifted Amy into her arms. The now-drowsy cox laid her head against Laura's shoulder and muttered, burrowing into her soft perch.

Laura glanced at the others in the room, realizing she'd get no help from them. She needed another pair of hands...

"Cass?"

"What?"

Laura's head snapped up at Cass's brittle tone. "Well, *your* happy juice certainly wore off fast. Mind opening your door for me?" She gestured with her chin as she settled Amy more comfortably in her arms.

Chagrined, Cass nodded. *Ease up Cass, jeez.* "Sorry, headache." She led Laura to the room she shared with Amy, wondering: if they were a couple, why Amy wasn't rooming with Laura? And why hadn't she known they were together? A few of the girls on the team were obviously couples and they all shared rooms. It wasn't team policy, but once the squad was settled, the roommate assignments generally got quietly shuffled as needed.

Cass realized that her coming had probably messed up Laura and Amy's plans.

"Look, if you want to room here, I can—"

Laura ducked under the low ceiling of the bunk bed and settled Amy gently on the bed. Amy immediately curled up facing the wall and began to snore softly. Laura turned and frowned at Cass, clearly puzzled by her comment. "Why would I want to do that?"

"Because you're...you and Amy...I mean, she said..." Crud. Maybe she *had* had too much rice wine at lunch. Laura was staring at her with the most peculiar expression coloring her classic features. She caught her breath as Laura grinned. *Wow, that smile packs a punch and a half. Shit.* Cass set her hand over her stomach to calm the butterflies suddenly flying around inside her.

With Amy snug under the covers, Laura sat gently on the side of the lower bunk, careful not to disturb the sleeping woman. She stared at Cass's flushed face, her gaze intense, then her eyes widened slightly in apparent realization. "Oh. I get it." Laura chuckled softly, the first sound of laughter Cass had heard from the usually quiet athlete. The rich, husky sound went straight through Cass, warming her from head to toe. "Amy and I aren't a couple. She's, ah, not my...well, let's just say that she prefers what I don't have." Laura cocked her head and studied Cass as Cass sat in the lone chair in the room, distinctly uncomfortable.

"Oh. I...oh." Cass's butterflies increased as Laura gazed at her. *Get a grip!* She waited a moment, willing the whirling in her stomach to subside while she scrambled for something intelligent to say. Laura unsettled her and the wine wasn't helping. In fact... "I think I'm going to...um, uh-oh."

Laura's eyes widened in alarm and she quickly grabbed Cass's shoulders and spun her toward the small bathroom shared with the room next door. Laura eased Cass to her knees and pulled her brown curls away from her face. For just a second Cass, despite the imminent eruption, was aware of Laura's fingers tangled in her hair, her grip supportive and gentle. Her stomach lurched again, but Cass wasn't sure if it was the drink or the fact that Laura's hand had slipped to the back of her neck in a near-caress.

Cass's whole body jerked at Laura's touch. "Go away, I don't need any help." Cass's words cut sharply through the air and Laura froze.

"I'm sorry?"

Mortified by her weakness and feeling her stomach rebelling even more, Cass was desperate to get Laura away. She hated being sick and hated even more that it was Laura witnessing her weakness. "I said, I don't need you. I just need to be left alone."

I just need to be left alone.

The words, combined with the stark whiteness of the small room and the ever-present, albeit faint smell of bleach seemed to trigger something in Laura. Cass's sharp command echoed through the small room as Laura reeled backward. Cass caught her breath, her own discomfort forgotten at the expression on Laura's face. It was as if Laura wasn't *here* with her anymore. She watched as Laura glanced wildly around, her eyes darting from the floor to the tub and back again. Sweat beaded on her face and her breathing grew rapid, shallow.

Cass jumped as Laura let out a low moan of pain, her face going the palest shade of white, her eyes far away. She pushed herself shakily to her feet as Laura stumbled back against the doorframe. She was afraid. Afraid to reach out and touch Laura. It was clear that Laura was not seeing her right now, and Cass was almost too afraid to know what she *was* seeing.

Despite her fear she reached out, easing toward Laura's shaking frame. Very softly, she said, "Laura, hey…"

With another low cry, Laura bolted from the room. Cass stumbled after her in time to see Laura push past the others in the common room and disappear down the hall. Coach Adler stepped into the room and strode to Cass's doorway. Cass could only stare at the coach, dumbstruck over what had just happened.

"What the hell was that?" Sheila's pointed question rose over the general confusion in the room.

Cass shook her head. "I...I don't know. I was...then she…" Cass swallowed hard against the rising tide inside her. "She was...

oh, God. I'm going to—" Cass spun and ran back into her room's bathroom just in time.

As she sat hunched over the toilet, she replayed over and over again the anguish on Laura's face. The pain. The same question rolled around in her head. "What *had* happened?" That question was followed by another. "How can I make it better?" Cass didn't know what to do with either question.

CHAPTER FOURTEEN

Tipping her head to shade her eyes against the glare of the setting sun, Cass leaned back on her elbows and watched the last of the crews practice for the day. She looked around as the teams finished. This really was a spectacular venue. The Shunyi Olympic Rowing-Canoeing Park had been built just for this event and it seemed to just flow with the scenery. She remembered her first view of the boathouse, with its undulating roof that mirrored the currents of the race causeway and the soothing, earth-toned colors of the walls and hallways. The permanent and floating docks, too, fit the space beautifully, offering an entry into the water without marring the line of the riverbanks. A spectacular place to compete. And to win.

A shout on the water pulled her attention back; the U.S. eight was on the water and nearing the finish line. Cass could just make out Amy's voice across the nearly still water, counting out the stroke she wanted her rowers to make as they practiced their "power tens;" the kick-it-into-gear stroke that could practically lift a shell out of the water and make it fly to the finish. It took a great deal of practice to get that synchronization right. Sweep rowing always looked odd to Cass. The idea of getting all eight women and all eight oars going at exactly the same time seemed an impossible task. Amy, an almost invisible red dot tucked into the stern of the boat, was taking the women through the transition from the racing rate to the higher-powered finish stroke rate. From Cass's perspective, it looked as if two of the women were having problems making a smooth transition. Cass wondered idly if Coach would have an alternate seat-race for one of the slots. That kind of intrasquad competition sometimes served as a wake-up call for rowers who were coasting along and letting the rest of the team carry them.

Cass closed her eyes and tilted her head back, enjoying the feel of the sun on her face and body. The light tank she'd put on after her earlier water training accented the muscles in her broad shoulders and the solid definition in her arms. Her white shorts came to mid-thigh and showcased the funny "rower's tan" that was the hazard of her racing unitard. She kicked off her sandals and buried her toes in the warm sand, enjoying the rare moment of inactivity. Every day since her arrival had been filled with introductions, to the other members of the team and to the coaches, assistants, trainers and doctors who made up the support aspect of their group or with intense training sessions. Everyone had been warm and welcoming, making her feel a part of the group almost from the first night.

One exception... Cass opened her eyes and tracked the U.S. boat as it came by for another pass. Seated in the number eight seat, the stroke seat, Laura set the rate for the crew according to Amy's instructions. Cass knew that Laura was on the money. Amy wouldn't rave about her if she were not right there when it counted. And Laura's record spoke for her capability: two National Championship medals in the eight and the four, along with her spectacular showing in the Pan Am Games last year. Personally, however... Cass shaded her eyes, trying to make out the features of the women out on the water.

Cass squirmed as she thought of the brief conversation they *had* managed four days ago in her dorm. *She probably thinks you're an idiot. Could you have acted any more like a rookie? First you assume she's sleeping with your roommate, then you kick her out when she's trying to help you not toss your cookies on the floor.* She wished she could have a do-over for that whole evening, starting with the first cup of rice wine Amy had given her.

Several times since, in the gym and as the team worked out together, Cass had looked up to discover Laura watching her. But when she'd offered a tentative smile, Laura would quickly look away. Despite their amicable dinner together during the team family night dinner, Laura remained an enigma. Cass did not know if she was simply shy or just very antisocial. Whichever, Cass had decided not to let Laura's attitude get to her. She was doing well here—she and Sarah were clicking as a team and she felt good about their prospects. They had less than two weeks to go before the start of the Games...the regatta...and it was coming together for them. That's what counted. Everything else was secondary as far as she was concerned.

Still...it bothered her. Something about Laura drew her, pulled at her. Cass found herself watching for her in the gym and in the village. Whenever the squad made plans to go somewhere, she unconsciously looked to Laura to see what she wanted to do. She didn't *want* to, she couldn't seem to help herself. Despite Laura's seeming antipathy toward her, Cass felt...something.

The eight was nearing the end of the causeway and this time Amy was guiding them toward the dock. With a small sigh Cass slipped her feet back into her sandals and stood, brushing the sand from her shorts. She had enough time for a quick workout before dinner, if she hustled. Maybe after that she'd try to track Laura down. Secondary or not, she hated being at odds with anyone, and she couldn't forget the look on Laura's face as she'd ordered her out of the room, and couldn't ignore the faint ache she felt because of it.

CHAPTER FIFTEEN

Cass stepped inside the blessedly cool facility and headed toward the gym her squad used most often. She heard voices coming through the open doorway and stopped just outside.

"Laura, what the hell is going on with you?" Coach's voice was low, intense.

Cass peeked around the doorway to see Laura standing rigid and angry, her back braced against the weight machine. Everything about her screamed "cornered." Neither woman saw her and Cass quickly eased back.

When Laura spoke, her voice was rough. "Nothing, Coach. I've got it covered."

"Like hell. You tore out of the dorm the other day so fast you nearly ran me down." Cass could imagine the coach running her hand through her hair, something she did often when she was frustrated. "Look. Is this about Shelly? That whole thing with Brenda? If it is—"

"No!" Laura's response was sharp, angry.

"Laura, look. I know it's been rough. I do. And you know I've got your back, one hundred percent. But...you've got to pull it together. The assistants are telling me you're out there biting the heads off of your crew. You're in the gym more than you're in the dorms...you can't keep this up."

"I can. I can do it and win."

Adler's sigh was audible even to Cass, hovering in the hallway. "Until last week I would have agreed with you. But now...Laura, you've got to talk to someone."

"I...I..." A long sigh echoed through the nearly empty room. Laura's next words were almost too quiet for Cass to hear. "Okay. I'm sorry, Coach. I'll talk to the doc tonight."

Adler's voice was calmer now, soothing. "Fine, I'll let her know you'll be stopping by."

The soft sound of the far door closing echoed through the room and Cass started. She eased back farther and stepped away from the half-open door, not wanting to be caught in the hallway. A rustle of movement stopped her and she found herself peeking forward again. Cass felt a jolt in the pit of her stomach.

Laura sat slumped on the bench of the machine her elbows resting heavily on her knees, and her head hanging low, the picture of dejection. She was muttering quietly to herself and Cass strained to hear her. "Get it together, Kelly. You don't need anyone, remember? You can do this. You *can* do this."

The words had an almost desperate ring to them, and Cass found herself aching for her teammate. Again Laura's soft voice reached her ears. This time Laura's voice was lower, weaker. It was clear she was fighting back tears.

"I don't know how, anymore. I am so tired...and I'm tired of doing it alone."

When the tears came, it was too much for Cass. She carefully and quietly eased back up the hallway and slipped through the door and out into the night. Laura's words had left her shaking and her tears had punched at Cass's gut, making Cass hurt in a way she hadn't thought possible anymore.

CHAPTER SIXTEEN

The boathouse was quiet and peaceful. Cass loved coming in here after everyone was gone for the day. Most of the lights were off and the rainbow of different colored shells from all over the world was muted by the night. She waved her credential at the tiny female Chinese guard and stepped inside, away from the heat and smell of the humid air outside. It was also relatively cooler in here and she sucked in the cleaner air with relief. The Chinese had built the new facility expressly for the Games and had included a circulating air system, something of a luxury compared to the boathouses she was used to. Boats lived on water, were built for moisture, but needed the dry docks to be just that, *dry*. Too much humidity in storage warped wood and torqued lean and clean designs. Cass didn't know how the Chinese had accomplished it; the air inside the boathouse was cool but not too cool and as dry as was possible despite the pervasive humidity.

She walked slowly among the racks of boats, enjoying the serenity of the neatly kept, echoing room. It always amazed her that while subtle changes had been made over the years to boat designs to enhance speed and fluidity through the water, the basic shape of the sculls was the same for everyone. Lighter materials, streamlined hulls, curved and cambered oar blades helped, but in the end it always came down to one thing: the athlete. If the athlete wasn't ready on the right day at the right time and the mental game wasn't there, it didn't matter how perfect the equipment, the boat wouldn't win.

Coming to the end of the row, Cass turned and moved along the concrete walkway. Lit by a single bulb hanging high above the aisle, the long shells disappeared into the darkness, adding to the air of mystery and silence in the cavernous space. A slight breeze carried with it the scents of fish, salt and sea that permeated every boathouse she knew. Mixed with that was the faint tang of the oils used to maintain the equipment of her sport. The thick, dark oil used on the slide runners to keep the seats moving smoothly within the shell mixed with the lighter oil for the gunnels and combined with the sweet smell of the wax some teams used on their shells to increase their speed. It all smelled like home to her. The familiar mixed with the new, all adding up to the friendly welcome-home boathouse aroma she so deeply loved.

Finding her own boat, Cass walked along, her fingers lightly trailing along the smooth, deep blue hull, her mind on the conversation she'd just overheard. She didn't know what was driving Laura, what demons were chasing her, but she could certainly understand about being alone. Alone was something Cass had dealt with for a long, long time.

She had friends, sure, and some closer than others. Here in Beijing she had made friends she was sure she'd have for the rest of her life. The experience they were sharing almost ensured that. But...deep inside, where it counted, she often felt alone. It was funny, Cass thought. In a country of more than one billion people, more now with the Olympians and their families and fans, she was alone.

It's a habit, she realized. *I don't know how not to be alone anymore.* After a year of focusing on herself and on her training, she didn't know how to let anyone in. Not *really* in, where it counted. Not that anyone was beating down the doors, but... *If someone, if Laura, wanted in, I don't know how. I—*

Thinking back to the night she and a few of the women had gone out to dinner, she bit back an automatic grimace of remembered embarrassment as Amy's words came back to her. "*Who's talking about love? We're talkin' wild, hot, monkey-sex.*"

Just the memory of that offhand comment made Cass flush and she jammed her hands into her pockets, heedless of the oily cloth in her hands. She wasn't a prude by any standard, she just didn't...hadn't...there'd been nobody she'd ever really wanted to get that close to. Maybe she really *had* been messed up by her crazy aunt and uncle and their "sex equals sin" diatribes. She couldn't imagine just...letting go and...well, letting *go.* And even if she wanted to, it wasn't like she had anyone she could just...approach. Even as she thought it, she closed her eyes as a memory flashed through. Laura, standing at the controls of the coach's launch, long, toned legs extending from worn shorts, her feet bare on the deck, the afternoon sun lighting her features and kissing her hair with fire.

Cass froze, her heart thudding in her chest. She sucked in a surprised breath and purposely stilled her thoughts. Taking a deep breath, she pulled her hands from her pockets and deliberately focused her attention on the long hull beneath her fingertips. *What am I thinking? There's nobody to let in and no reason to. It's clear that Laura's got her own issues, and big ones. I don't need that. I have a goal, and I have a plan.* Somehow her own thoughts rang false in her head. She relentlessly shoved that afternoon memory away, slamming the door behind it.

Cass wandered aimlessly out of the back door of the boathouse, down the ramp and onto the dock. She bounced once, twice, enjoying the springy feel as it rested on the water. The dock was anchored in place by the pilings jutting out from the bed of the man-made river. She walked to the end and sat, her back against the tall piling, her toes dangling in the dark water below. A soft breeze blew up the course from the ocean, lifting her sweat-dampened hair from her neck. She turned her face toward the breeze and lay back, gazing at the stars. Small and large, faint and bright, they winked at her, moving in their slow dance across the sky as she lay on the dock. Alone.

CHAPTER SEVENTEEN

Breathing deeply and trying to ignore the ever-present heaviness in the air, Cass ignored the voices of the men behind her and turned left, back toward the village. She grinned as she heard the men whistle and call, not understanding the words, but understanding the tone. She passed these same old men every day and every day they called out to her in Chinese. It was harmless and while she was not sure if they were cheering her on or inviting her to stop and visit, she had begun to look forward to hearing them at the end of her daily runs. It was darker now, she was out later than she'd intended. She picked up her pace, wanting to get back to the athletes village part of the residential section before full dark. She was not afraid of running alone, but she was not stupid enough to invite danger either. While most of the city was caught up in the kinship and brotherhood of the Olympic spirit, she was not naive enough to believe that everyone here was harmless.

The sound of a second pair of shoes slapping against the pavement behind her caught her attention and she glanced back over her shoulder, startled to see a flash of blue illuminated by the lights spilling out of the open doorways on the street. Uneasy now, Cass picked up her pace and took the last turn toward her building, choosing a busier street than she usually did just to be safe. Behind her she heard the steps of her pursuer coming closer. She slowed, tensed up and prepared to defend herself, preferring to fight on her own terms rather than be surprised on someone else's. Despite her preparations, a breathless voice behind Cass threw her off her stride.

"You should be careful, running alone at night."

The last voice she had expected to hear was Laura's. Cass recovered quickly. "Yeah, I guess. But, I'm not running alone now, am I?" Winded from the run and the additional adrenaline, she saw Laura adjust her pace to her own shorter stride as Laura pulled even with her. "You don't have to run with me, you know. We're almost there."

"I don't mind."

"Suit yourself."

Tired from her run and of her teammate's short, almost dismissive responses, Cass was unusually abrupt herself. Since the day Laura had picked her up at the airport, the lanky rower had made an effort, or so it seemed to Cass, to avoid any sort of communication with her that might be construed as friendly. Every attempt Cass made was cut short or simply ignored.

Last week's episode over the toilet had been humiliating. More so because Laura had been the one to witness her misery. Cass was embarrassed both by her behavior that night and the fact that she'd been rude to Laura, sending her away without even a thank you for helping both her and Amy when they'd needed it.

Amy had recovered from their overindulgence with no lasting effects, while Cass had paid dearly for her experiment with the local fermented drinks. Coach had required extra practices the next day, and Cass was certain it was because she'd been aware of the women's adventures with the rice wine. Despite her embarrassment, Cass had been determined to find and thank Laura for her help and to apologize for being rude. However, every time she'd tried, Laura had found an excuse to leave, or had simply avoided being near enough to Cass to talk. It was frustrating, annoying, but tonight it was bothering her more than it should.

Maybe it was the conversation she'd overheard between Coach and Laura, maybe it was her own nerves about the upcoming heats. Whatever it was, Cass's normal good nature wasn't serving her tonight. *Let it go Cass, you don't have to be everybody's friend. It'd be nice to get more than two words from her though. She's...interesting.* Despite Laura's abruptness and apparent unwillingness to even be polite, Cass had found herself watching the rower at odd times during the day. There was something about her that drew Cass, and while she was not clear on what to do about it, she was pretty clear on the fact that Laura did not seem to have any interest in her, professionally or personally. While the professional aspect pricked her ego a bit, the personal side and her own reaction to it perplexed her. It wasn't like Cass to be fixated on someone, especially someone who showed no interest in return.

As they neared the front of their building, Laura gave Cass a brief nod and stopped along the front pathway to stretch, breathing deeply as she windmilled her arms and shook out her legs. Cass glanced at the enigmatic rower, but said nothing as she, too, began her post-run stretching and cool down. Lying on the grass, she bent one leg behind her and leaned back, trying to ease a growing cramp in her calf. It was in her bad leg and because she'd pushed a little harder than usual at the end of her run, she was feeling the pain. Shifting again, Cass grunted as the calf seized up entirely, the muscles beneath her scar going into a spasm she knew wouldn't end soon without help.

"Damn."

"You okay?"

"Yeah. I...damn. No." Reluctantly, she looked up at Laura, appreciating even through the pain in her leg the beauty of the woman before her, washed into black and white by the night and the artificial illumination around them. "I know you're not crazy about me, but I could use a hand here. Charley horse."

"Sure." Ignoring the hand Cass was holding up, Laura instead bent and ran her hands down Cass's leg. "It's this one, right?"

"Uh..." Cass stuttered, her brain skipping to a halt as Laura's warm hands enveloped her calf. "Yeah, it's right—"

"Shh, yeah, I know, I can feel it. Hard as a rock. Lean back, okay?" Laura gently raised Cass's leg, her green eyes dark as Cass fell backward onto the grass. Laura slid her hands up along the calf, fingers lightly tracing the crisscrossing scar tissue and feeling the knotted muscle underneath the surface. She began to push Cass's toes upward, forcing the muscle to stretch. Laura gently extended the muscle, her long fingers brushing the keloid scarring that twisted up the leg. Cass watched as Laura's eyes followed the path of her fingers and for the first time in a long while, found herself wanting to explain the scarring. Then Laura's grip shifted and she ran her fingers along the back of Cass's calf, working to ease the spasm. Below her, Cass gasped in pain, but nodded at Laura's questioning look.

"Yeah, keep going." Despite the pain, Cass was very aware of Laura's hands on her skin. Moreover, she was aware of her reaction to those hands.

"I um..." Laura stammered as she kept pushing Cass's foot upward, waiting for the muscle to release beneath her fingers. "Look, I'm sorry if I gave you the impression that I don't like you. I don't know how you got that idea."

Grunting as her muscles fought against Laura's manipulation of them, Cass grimaced. "Yeah okay. Must've been my mistake, then." Aggravated by both the pain and Laura's attitude of the last weeks, Cass let her frustrations loose. "You don't know how could I have gotten that idea? Maybe when you ditched me at the airport?" She shifted slightly, finally feeling the tense knot begin to relax. "Could it be because you've not spoken to me more than twice, until tonight? Or, wait, maybe because I got drunk, sick and threw you—"

"Okay. Okay." Laura gently let Cass's leg fall forward, still massaging the scarred calf. "I guess I was a bit...standoffish. Sorry."

"Standoffish? Wow, do you have a gift for understatement."

Relieved to have the knotted muscle loosened again and aware of the flushing warmth filling her at Laura's touch, Cass pulled her leg from Laura's hands. She was not being fair and she knew it. She was covering her unexpected reaction to Laura's touch with a biting sarcasm that wasn't normally her style. Belatedly remembering her plan to thank Laura for her help the week before, Cass was embarrassed all over again. "I'm sorry, too. Um, and about last week, I—"

Laura cut her off. "Let's just forget about last week, all right?" Laura extended her hands again, offering Cass help up. She grimaced and added, "I'd just rather not talk about it."

Cass waved her hands away. "No, wait. I can't just forget it. I was rude to you when you were trying to help me." She looked up at Laura. "The worst part is that I felt..." She stopped and bit her lip. "I felt like I hurt your feelings and...well, I'm sorry."

Laura just stood there, gazing at her, her expression blank. Cass waited a moment and shrugged, then looked away. *Okay, well, that went well. Guess she really did want to just forget about it.* She grimaced as she began to stand; despite her efforts, her calf was cramping again.

"Here. It'll be easier if I help you, okay?" Laura squatted and reached again for Cass's hands. "It's okay, really. You didn't hurt my feelings. And...*I* apologize. I didn't mean to make you feel unwelcome."

Cass slipped her hands into Laura's and gingerly stood. With Laura holding her steady she flexed her leg again, her attention slipping from the pain in her leg to the warmth of the fingers holding hers. Warm and dry and larger than Cass's, with the calluses that marked every rower's hands, Laura's enveloped Cass's own without restricting them. *Hands...hands are always my weakness. I love hands.*

Cass shook her head when she found herself staring down at their entangled fingers. It was time for a hot shower and some food before heading to bed, she decided. *When you start soliloquizing about hands...jeez.* "Look, I'm tired, hungry, hurting and nervous as hell about next week. So...apology accepted." Cass, pulling her hands free, bent and stretched one last time, and then started toward the doors of their building. "I really did feel as though you'd ditched me at the airport, though."

Laura pulled her cap off and ran her fingers through her hair, freeing her curls from their restricting band. "No, I'm the one who's sorry. I have a lot on my mind and it's not just the stuff here. I guess I let it spill over." She opened the door to their building and waved to the guard at the desk. "Can we start again?" Holding out her hand, she smiled at Cass. "Hi, I'm Laura. Nice to meet you, welcome to Beijing." She paused, then added, "And welcome to the team."

Cass stepped into the elevator as Laura held the door, then shook the proffered hand. She grinned up at Laura and gently tightened her grip. "Hi, I'm Cass. Nice to meet you."

Both women were smiling as the elevator doors slid shut.

CHAPTER EIGHTEEN

Cass jerked awake as the van came to a stop outside of the village dining hall. This morning's workout had been brutal and she was almost too tired to move from the seat.

"C'mon Cass, time to put food in you." Amy nudged her shoulder.

"Can't. Too tired to eat."

Amy nudged her again. "Cass...c'mon. I can't get out until you do."

"Fine, just quit pushing, will ya?"

Sliding along the seat, Cass crouched and stepped out of the van. Instead of meeting the expected curb, her foot met only open air. With a yelp, she twisted and reached out, startled to feel a strong arm snake around her waist, stopping her fall. Laura's warm voice filled her ears, and Cass opened her eyes to find Laura's face inches from her own.

"I've got you."

"Uh...oh. Thanks."

"Wouldn't do to have you get hurt, I think we've run out of spares."

Cass fought to catch her breath. *You can't breathe because she's got a grip on your abdomen. Yeah, that's it. Sure. Keep telling yourself that, Cass. Liar.*

"Thanks...um, you can let go now, you know."

Laura's arm stayed where it was for a moment, locked around Cass's waist, her other arm bracing the weight of the two of them against the van. The rest of the team had gone on ahead of them. Laura smiled again at Cass before letting her go.

"I did promise, did I not, to try to be nicer? How am I doing?"

Slightly breathless from the sudden warm smile on Laura's face and the warm things that smile was doing to her insides, Cass just nodded.

"Cass? You okay?"

Cass shook her head a bit to clear it. "Yeah. Fine. I think I just need food."

"Let's get you inside then."

"Sure."

Slightly bemused, Cass followed Laura inside. *Food. Yeah. That's what you need. Whoa.*

Cass spent the rest of the dinner trying to conquer the butterflies racing around her stomach. Butterflies that multiplied each time she looked up to see Laura watching her.

CHAPTER NINETEEN

Four days later Cass stepped from the bathroom, toweling her hair dry to find Amy grumbling and tossing her sheets and pillowcases into a pile on the bed. It was unusually warm in the room and Cass automatically headed toward the air conditioning controls to adjust the temperature.

"Don't bother. Frigging thing doesn't work anymore."

"You're joking."

"Uh-uh. Coach says it'll be at least a week before they can get it fixed. I swear we got the only building here that's older than the Imperial Palace and the air conditioner is almost as old." With a final yank, Amy's corner sheet came free and she stumbled back into Cass. "Sorry."

Cass shook out her hair and began combing through it. "So, what's the deal? Are you going to sleep on the beach?" She grinned at the thought, figuring Amy would have several offers of sleeping companion if she wished, and pictured her spunky roommate telling her would-be suitors where to get off.

"Ha, not likely. No, Coach suggested we all move to the common room. The air still works in there...mostly and it'll be cooler."

"Yeah, until we all get in there." With a shrug, Cass threw on a tank top and her oldest cotton shorts, fondly rubbing the fading ink of Bucky Badger as he strutted across her thigh. "We're taking the mattresses, right?"

"Yeah, we'll come back for them after we stake out our space. I'm leaving my clothes and uniforms in here, just to change and stuff."

"I'll meet you out there." Cass began pulling her own bedding off, a more difficult task with her upper bunk. Laura's voice startled her from the doorway.

"Hey. I see you both got the 'evac' notice." Laura watched Cass struggle with her sheets before reaching over her to pull the bedcovers free. "Better?"

"Yeah. Thanks." Aware that she had nothing on under her shirt or her shorts, Cass was suddenly grateful for the increasing warmth in the room...and the fact that she'd opted for a dark tank top and not the white she'd been about to grab.

In the days since their "do-over" in the elevator, Laura had made a noticeable effort to be friendlier and Cass was enjoying Laura's emerging sense of humor and personality. Really enjoying it. She knew herself well enough to know that she was attracted to Laura, a fact she'd admitted to herself and to Amy late last night. Amy had been delighted and had surprised Cass by not teasing her, as she'd expected, but offering what information she felt she could share about their teammate.

A crush was one thing, but waltzing around in front of the object of her affection in almost nothing was another. *I'm gonna poke out enough in this shirt and with her standing so close all I need is cold air to make the effect complete!* Crossing her arms somewhat defensively over her chest, she asked, "Are, uh, you all settled out there?"

"Just about." Laura scratched her head, shifting her weight

from one foot to another. “Um, I’ve snagged some room near one of the windows with screens on them...” Laura hesitated, then took a deep breath and added. “There’s probably enough room for you to toss your mattress there, if you’d like. That way if the A/C in the main room dies too, we’ll at least catch a breeze.”

Raising her eyes to meet Laura’s, Cass studied her face, noting the dark ring around the green of Laura’s eyes and enjoying the deeper color in the softly lit room.

“You’re really taking this ‘being nicer’ plan to heart.”

“Yeah, well, turning over a new leaf and all.”

“I appreciate it. And the window space, if you have the room.”

Laura simply smiled and nudged Cass out of the way, reaching for the mattress on the upper bunk. “I’ll get this while you get your bedding.”

“Lead the way.” Cass smiled at Amy as the cox came back into the room for her second load.

Amy looked from Cass to Laura and back again, tossing a wink Cass’s way. “Hey! How’d you rate the manual laborer?”

Cass grinned back. “Just lucky, I guess.”

CHAPTER TWENTY

"Mind if I join you?"

Laura's soft voice startled Cass out of her reverie. Cass had come into the rec center in the residential area of the Olympic Village to check her e-mail and to simply relax. Despite Amy's claims to the contrary, the dorms, like the rest of the village, were brand new. Whatever was affecting the air conditioning was also disrupting the Internet service in the dorms. It didn't seem to be affecting the other areas, however, and the main recreational area for the athletes was state-of-the-art. The Internet café sported docking stations, desktop units and offered wireless for those who could access it. The café was crowded, but not overly so and Cass had quickly found an overstuffed chair with her name on it. She'd come here directly after the morning's training sessions, looking for a chance to catch up on her mail. And...maybe to lose herself in the larger crowd for a while.

The other night, as she'd sat on the dock, Cass had felt very alone, despite the welcome from her teammates. Now, with the entire team packed into one common room, "loneliness," at least in the traditional sense, was unheard of. For someone who was used to her quiet time, the sudden enforced closeness was grating on her nerves. So she'd used her rare free time to hunt up one of the more commercial spaces in the village. It was quite possible to be alone in a busy Starbucks if you wanted to be. Her little correspondence had not taken much time to answer and Cass had simply lost herself in idly watching the ebb and flow of the crowd.

As more teams transitioned to Beijing from their temporary training facilities in Japan or other locations, the population of the Olympic Village was growing. Eventually nearly eighteen thousand athletes and team officials would fill the residential section, located on the western side of the enormous, nearly two-hundred-acre facility the Chinese had named the Olympic Green. Adjoining the village was the even larger Forest Park, a nineteen-hundred-acre mix of lakes, pathways and manicured lawns designed to "soothe the eyes and ease the soul" according to the brochure she'd read. Cass had not yet made it to the main park, and she was beginning to feel the strain of being among so many people in one concentrated area. Laura's interruption made her realize she had been in the café longer than she'd intended.

"What time is it?" Cass asked.

"Close to three."

"Oh man. Really? Have I missed anything?" Cass flipped her laptop closed and began tossing her things into her backpack.

"Relax. No, nothing. Remember? Coach gave us the afternoon off. Furlough for 'good behavior' I think she called it." She cocked her head slightly to one side. "I hear John Sullivan's looking for you."

They both laughed at that. Sarah's father had taken to calling Cass his "other girl" when introducing the double scull team around. Cass wasn't entirely certain how she felt about it, though it was clear that John meant it in a fun, family way.

Laura unknowingly echoed Cass's thoughts. "I wouldn't worry about it. Big John sort of adopts all of the team's orphans."

"Oh, right." Cass continued to pack her backpack, deciding she'd spent enough time inside today. Maybe she'd check out the larger Forest Park.

"So, what were you up to?"

"Just checking e-mail, nothing much."

"Keeping the family up to date?"

"Ahh." Cass shifted uncomfortably. "No."

"I'm sorry, I didn't mean to pry."

"It's okay, you're not prying. There's just no family to keep updated." Cass stood up and considered her companion for a moment. At Laura's look, she waved a hand toward the door. "It's getting crowded in here, want to take a walk? Or were you just looking for the chair?"

"Sure. I figured I'd roust you out and scope out the room." Laura quirked a small smile at Cass. "But, seeing as all the interesting people are leaving, I guess a walk sounds good."

Leaving the crowded shop behind, the two women headed away from the village center. Because they were still in the residential area of the Olympic Village, most of those around them were athletes, coaches and support staff. It made for an intense group of people, and Cass decided she needed a break—from all things Olympic. Just for a short while. She glanced over at Laura then hesitated while she considered the last few days.

True to her word, Laura had indeed reserved a spot for her near the windows in their common room, but then she had withdrawn again. While Cass had hoped that the enforced proximity would give them a chance to talk more, the more she attempted to get to know her, the more Laura closed up. Cass could see that Laura was trying, but whatever held her back was winning. In the week since the move to the common room, they'd had hardly a minute together that didn't directly involve rowing. Cass wanted to spend some time getting to know this intriguing woman, but spending her off-time with Cass didn't seem high on Laura's list of priorities. Well, except for today. On the other hand—

"You look like a guppy."

"Sorry?"

"You keep opening and closing your mouth, but nothing's coming out. Are you having trouble breathing or are you practicing your fish impressions?"

Cass chuckled, her indecisiveness gone. She pulled Laura off the crowded sidewalk.

"I found this neat little park, just outside of the residential area, want to go?"

"Sounds great, if you don't mind the company."

"No, it's fine. You're fine, I mean. It's not as big, or so I hear, as that huge Forest Park, but it's a pretty neat place. I guess all of this was just dirt and rubble until January or so, from what I've read. The park, though, I think it's been here a while. It's a bit of a walk."

Laura shrugged. "I'm game if you are, we've got the rest of the day free."

Fifteen minutes later, Cass waved Laura through a small rusted gate on the edge of the official Olympic property. Tucked into an aged stone wall, the entrance nearly blended into the shadows. The gate creaked softly as Laura pushed it closed behind them, the latch making a muffled clang. Inside the garden the afternoon sun's rays filtered through the leaves, dotting the ground and stone statues with dancing waves of light and dark. Fifty or so yards from the entrance, the ground rose abruptly—a steep hillside covered with trees, brush and brilliant flowers.

Laura took a deep breath. The rich scents of flowers and mulch, along with the silence of the enclosed yard, was heady. "This is so cool, how did you find it?"

"I was out running about two weeks ago, trying to get used to the heavy air and smog and I just kind of stumbled on it."

They shared a grimace as they crossed the spongy grass. The legendary dirty air of China had lived up to its reputation, despite assurances from the various Olympic officials. The smog was one of the reasons the U.S. team had chosen to train in Japan until transitioning to Beijing just a week before Cass joined them.

Cass led them to a small stone bench that looked as if it

had grown up under the ancient tree that shaded it. Dappled in grays, greens and blacks, the carvings on the bench were worn with time, nearly invisible to the eye and barely discernible to searching fingers.

Laura sat and leaned back, resting against the gnarled tree trunk, and Cass watched her close her eyes in apparent appreciation. In here, the noise and bustle of the busy city outside seemed far away. Even the ever-present smog seemed less dense. The damp smell of the grass, combined with the musty smell of whatever the caretakers used to mulch the flower beds, and the flowers themselves, hung in the air, but was not oppressive. It was wonderful.

"What is this place? Are we in somebody's garden?" Laura opened her eyes and looked up at Cass.

"Miu, over in the gym? She said it's a park and really, I've checked all around. That's the only entrance. It's called 'Xiangshan.' Miu says it means 'fragrant hills.' I think she's right, it smells incredible in here, doesn't it?"

Cass sat on the ground, resting her back against the bench, one shoulder just brushing Laura's leg. She leaned her head back and studied the steep hillside that climbed away toward the sky. She pointed out what she knew of the park. "Miu called the trees with the fan-shaped leaves ginkgo and the others are called smoke trees. She says they turn amazing shades of orange and gold in the autumn."

"You and Miu seem to be chatting a lot."

"She's been great. She helped me get settled and made sure the other equipment guys knew where to put my stuff."

"Yeah, she did the same for the team when we got here."

They sat together in silence, Cass enjoying the opportunity to simply relax and *be*. The gentle perfume of the blooming trees and flowers bathed them in sweet, aromatic waves as the breeze filtered through the little park. In the comfortable silence, Cass was acutely aware of where her shoulder rested against Laura's knee, of the warmth she felt through the thin material of her polo shirt. She liked the connection and was careful not to move too much as she settled her back more comfortably against the bench. She hadn't been looking for company today, had, in fact, been trying to avoid it. But now she was glad that company had found her. That it had been Laura who'd found her.

"Hey Cass?"

"Mmm?" Cass's voice was sleepy as Laura's soft voice pulled her from her thoughts.

"This is perfect, thanks for sharing it with me."

"My pleasure."

"Mind if I ask you something?"

"Mmm. Nope, but I get a question in exchange."

Cass felt Laura's knee move against her shoulder, and she looked up to see Laura's green eyes sparkling down at her. *You hate personal discussions, dummy, and you just opened yourself up for one.* But, surprisingly, in this case she didn't seem to mind. As long as it was Laura doing the asking.

"Fair enough, I guess." Laura hesitated for a long moment before speaking. "What's the deal with your family? I mean, I guess I expected that you'd have lots of family here, or at least at home, cheering you on."

"Wow, ask an easy question, why don't you?" Taking a chance, Cass shifted her back away from the bench leg and rested it fully against Laura's softer legs. She crossed her legs and idly began shredding a fallen leaf.

"Um. Sorry. Bad subject. Never mind."

Cass twisted and caught the look of embarrassment on Laura's face. She felt bad for shutting her down. It was the first time Laura had initiated any real conversation and she'd blown it. *Suck it up, Cass.* She took a deep breath and allowed herself to enjoy the warmth of Laura's legs against her back before speaking. "It's okay I guess. I don't have a dad. Well, I suppose I did, but I mean I don't know who he is. My mom..."

Cass's voice caught and Laura lifted her head from where it lay resting against the tree behind them. She reached out and rested her hand on Cass's hair, and Cass leaned into the touch. The pain she felt warred with the peace of the garden and Cass resented the intrusion.

"I'm sorry, Cass. You don't have to talk about it."

"Um—" Cass cleared her throat. She spoke in short, brief sentences. It was easier to say it in shorter bursts. "No. It's fine.

My mom. She's an alcoholic. I haven't seen her since I was eight. She left me in our apartment one night and just...disappeared. Social services came. I think a neighbor complained of the smell or something. Anyway, they shipped me off to my uncle and his wife."

Saying nothing, Laura sat, her fingers gently playing with the curl that had tumbled across her knuckle. Cass let her head fall backward, silently encouraging Laura's touch, sighing slightly as she continued.

"They had two kids, my uncle and aunt. Have two kids I mean. Carl, he's forty-something now. I haven't heard from him in ages. He used to...well, let's say he made it his mission in life to know I was unwanted in *his* house. I guess he's married with kids of his own by now, God help them." Cass swallowed and leaned into Laura's gentle massage. "Nancy was the other kid. She was closer to my age, a year older. She was nice at first, but after Carl got to her a few times...well, it wasn't pleasant. She e-mails me now, sometimes. We sort of got back in touch after my accident. I'm surprised she even knew about it, to be honest. And, to complete the picture, there's my uncle, Marty, and his wife, Lisa. They were not at all pleased to have another mouth to feed, let alone the 'no-good kid of that loser, waste of a sister' of his. Toss in the last damning feature, me being gay." Cass shrugged slightly. "I think me being a lesbian sort of vindicated them in some way: 'Blood will out' as my uncle says." Cass was silent for a few minutes, then cleared her throat and lifted her head. She turned and caught Laura's eye. "So, there you have it." She shrugged, her expression saying it all.

"I'm sorry."

"It's not your fault."

"Yeah, I know. But I'm sorry anyway." Laura swallowed, clearly angry. "How does someone throw away the gift of a beautiful child?" She shook her head. Her fingers clenched before she blew out a deep breath, her hands relaxing as she breathed out. As her hand stretched, her fingers tangled again in the ends of Cass's hair. "I am sorry if talking about it made you upset."

"It doesn't, not any more. It was a long time ago." Cass knew that the tension in her voice belied her words, but really, it was the thing to say, wasn't it?

"Still. I *am* sorry." Laura smiled down at her, her expression more open than any other time Cass had seen it. There was no pity there, only...concern. Concern for her, Cass, and that simple look helped. After a moment, Laura asked, "Um, how...well, how did you end up..."

"Here? Rowing? I worked my ass off. Actually, I left my uncle's when I was sixteen. I talked my way into a job at Camp Randall, the football stadium near the University of Wisconsin. After a few months of going back and forth from the farm to town, I talked a friend of mine from school—she was two years older—into getting an apartment. We shared expenses. I went to school and worked like crazy. Pretty soon I was working in the sports medicine office and I loved it. The PTs were great and the team trainers hung out there." Cass shrugged. "I worked hard, some of the trainers wrote me nice letters and I got a scholarship to the UW."

"You rowed as an undergrad? How come we never met? Cal always thinks of Wisco as 'little sisters.'"

"Well, I didn't really row till grad school, that was eight years after my degree. And," Cass stopped, doing the math, "I'm a few years older than you are, I think, so..."

"How old are you?"

"I'll be thirty-one in a few weeks."

"Hmm. Happy birthday, early."

"Thanks."

"You're not that much older, I'm only three behind you. Guess it was enough, though."

Cass shifted again, pulling her knees up and wrapping her arms around them. She turned herself and resettled her shoulder against Laura's knees, accidentally dislodging Laura's hand from her head in the process, and immediately missing the contact. She took a deep breath and blew it out slowly, focusing on the sounds of the garden around them. A small animal rustled the bushes nearby and a slight breeze moved the leaves above them, changing the shadows dancing below. Laura moved her leg slightly and Cass looked back at her. "I get one now, you know."

"One what?"

"One question." Cass twisted and rested her arm across the bench seat. She rested her chin against her fingers and raised an eyebrow in challenge. "Fair's fair."

Laura's eyes caught Cass's and a slow smile spread across her face, and the effect was immediate. Cass's heart sped up. The low afternoon sun lit the leaves around them, and the color brought out the intense green of Laura's eyes. *Oh, man. I need to back up here. I could get really, really lost in those eyes.* She took a steadying breath and returned the smile, wondering at the almost hesitant expression on Laura's face. Laura shrugged and gave a faint wink.

"Sure. Bring it."

Cass studied her, searching Laura's expression. Laura returned her gaze evenly, her expression curious, and just a tiny bit wary. She jumped when Cass suddenly stood and held out her hand. Automatically Laura reached out and let her companion tug her to her feet.

"Hungry?"

"That's your question? What a waste. I'm disappointed in you."

Cass heard the tiny note of relief in Laura's voice. "Nope. That didn't count. I'm saving up." She stood still, aware that her hand was still holding Laura's. She felt like a schoolgirl on her first date, but she really didn't want to let go. She waited for Laura to pull her hand free and was surprised when Laura instead swung their hands back and forth, pulling Cass back toward the gate. "Fine then. Save it up, 'cause yes, I'm hungry."

Cass kept her hand in Laura's as they headed back to the residential area. As they walked, she considered the opportunity to ask Laura anything. Could she...did she dare ask about what she'd overheard in the gym? She didn't want to risk their fledgling connection, but... Glancing up at the relaxed expression on Laura's face, Cass tabled the idea for now, unwilling to ask anything that might chase away their enjoyment of the afternoon.

CHAPTER TWENTY-ONE

"Hey, give me a hand with this, would you?" Sheila Adler called out to the room in general, hoping someone was inside to lend a hand.

Cass looked up from her book and quickly jumped up and ran over to hold open the door. Boxes of all sizes threatened to wobble free of her grasp, and Cass tripped over the jumble of mattresses on the floor in an effort to save them. Together she and Sheila carried their load to the small TV alcove just off the main room, stacking the boxes against the walls. Sheila grunted as she dropped the largest of the packages to the floor. She placed her hands on her hips and leaned back, forcing her back to audibly pop. She smiled as Cass winced. As awful as they sounded, they both knew how good those bone-cracking stretches could be. Sheila glanced around as they returned to the common room.

"Holy cow. You guys certainly have moved in out here." Mattresses, mostly unmade, were strewn around the room, tucked into every available nook and cranny. Some grouped in pairs, others single and one or two set apart from the rest, the room was a patchwork quilt of bedding and pillows.

"It's been weird, but okay. At least there's air here. I'll bet the guys don't have to go through this."

Sheila scratched her head and shook it in disgust. "No, dammit. Their dorms are perfect. It's only us and the Dutch, and let me tell you, they're pretty pissed. The coaches' launches have better A/C than your dorms," she muttered, wiping her brow. She was referring to the large, shallow-draft boats she and her assistants used to coach the teams while on the water.

Sheila dropped tiredly onto one of the overstuffed chairs, propping up her feet on the edge of a nearby footrest. Toeing off her sneakers, the coach leaned her head back against the seat with a sigh. She glanced over to where Cass was folding herself into a corner of the long couch.

"How about you? How are you holding up?"

"You mean with the dorm thing?" Cass shrugged one shoulder. "Fine, I guess. It's not really an issue. I mean, at night when I'm here, I sleep, you know? I'm so wasted by the end of the day that it would take a lot to wake me."

"Good." Sheila lifted her head to study Cass, quietly assessing her.

Her long, measuring look didn't pass unnoticed, and Cass met her gaze squarely, her expression open. "What?"

"Nothing." Sheila dropped her head back again. "Okay, not 'nothing,' but it's not anything. I want to know how *you're* doing. With the training, with the team, with...adjusting. You kind of hit the ground running here, and I haven't had as much chance as I'd like to talk." She tilted her head from side to side, stretching her neck and enjoying the rare opportunity to just sit and relax with one of her athletes.

An Olympian herself, "back in the day," as her charges occasionally teased her, Sheila was well acquainted with the pressure her women were under every day. The scrutiny of not only members of the international press, but also the sponsors, the coaches, their own families, and, perhaps most of all, themselves. Nobody was harder on an athlete than the athlete herself. That's what made them who they were. The best of the elite. "Gods and goddesses among us," as one newspaper headline proclaimed this morning. Walking examples of what everyone aspired to be. Young, fit, beautiful and perfect, or as near as possible, specimens of humanity at its finest. Too bad everyone around them wasn't as...pure. Or as good an example. Sheila waited for Cass to answer her question, and when it was apparent that she wouldn't, Sheila tried again. "So, really. How are you? I really want to know, Cass." She waved a carefully lazy hand toward Cass. "You, the leg, how's your head. Are you in the game? Ready to go? Anything I should know about?"

She dropped her arm to her side and waited. One of the hardest things she'd had to learn as a coach was how to get her athletes to open up. To admit to...needing. They were, all of them, and she counted herself among them in this case, such classic type A's. Driven, determined, goal-oriented. So focused on the result that the "self" often fell by the wayside. Getting any of them to come to her was sometimes like pulling teeth, and she knew instinctively that Cass Flynn fit that type to a T. So she sat bonelessly in the chair, very much alert and waiting for Cass's answer, her eyes mostly closed, carefully keeping still. She didn't yet have a handle on Cass, but she really needed to know how the newest team member was doing, both professionally *and* personally. She didn't move as Cass stretched and flexed her leg, instead watching the limb move smoothly despite the massive scarring that crisscrossed the tanned skin.

"Oh." Cass was quiet for a minute, then spoke up again. Her words were slow to come, almost hesitant. "I'm fine. Honestly. The leg's good—better, in fact, than I would have thought possible, given the amount of work we've been doing. I feel good here...*right*, you know?"

"Mmm hmm."

"I mean, yeah, the first few days were a bit...rocky, but now... yeah, I'm good."

"Good." Sheila would take "good," for now. She was mostly listening to what Cass *didn't* say. Rather, how she sounded. And to Sheila's mind, Cass sounded, well, *good.* Confident, relaxed, or as much as was possible in this highly charged atmosphere. They sat together in silence for a few more minutes before Sheila grunted and pulled herself upright. "Well, since you're so 'good,'" and she made air quotes as she stretched again and shot a teasing look at Cass. "You can help me sort out some things."

"Um, sure. Are we talking literally or figuratively?"

"Literally. Come on. Our racing uniforms just came. Took them long enough, these things were supposed to be delivered before we transitioned to Beijing. Give me a hand separating them out, would you?"

"Oh, very cool. I've been looking forward to getting mine."

In tandem, they opened boxes and began the sorting process. After a minute Cass spoke up, "You know, I realize it's probably really nerdy, but...well, I'm really excited to get the uniform." She blushed, the color rising up her fair skin.

Sheila raised an eyebrow at Cass, smiling at the bright flush coloring Cass's face and neck.

Cass shrugged. "I know, sorry. I keep expecting it to...I don't know, wear off. Usually it's the rookies who go gaga over their uniforms. At this level, we're supposed to be, well, over it, I guess."

"It's not nerdy, and I'll tell you a secret. No less than nine of your teammates have asked me when these were going to arrive." Sheila glanced around at the empty if cluttered room then leaned in to say conspiratorially, "And, truth time here, I still get an incredible thrill when I put on the team jacket." Slightly embarrassed herself, Sheila's shrug echoed Cass's earlier one. "What can I say? I love wearing that Team USA logo."

Cass looked at Sheila, "It never gets old, does it?"

"It hasn't yet."

The two exchanged companionable smiles as they continued their work. Sheila was glad that it had been Cass she'd found to help her. She had a better handle on her now, a better understanding of how Cass fit with the whole.

For the next two hours, Cass helped Sheila sort the long-awaited uniforms. She bagged and labeled as Sheila called out names and tossed the Lycra unitard and accompanying shorts, polo shirt and jacket toward her. The two chatted about the upcoming races and their primary competition, and Cass enjoyed the opportunity to get to know her coach a bit more. Finally, with everything bagged and awaiting the return of the athletes from their free afternoon, Cass grabbed a bottle of water for each of them and led Sheila out onto the roof.

"I love coming up here, smog and all." She settled herself on the low wall that bordered the rooftop, her legs dangling over the edge. "Welcome to my space."

"Quite a view." Sheila leaned forward and peered over the edge before stepping back to look over the city and newly landscaped parkland before her.

"Yeah." Cass pointed out the landmarks she knew. "Over there's the restaurant block." She laughed quietly. "I have to say, I haven't been able to find much in the way of real Chinese food, other than the place Sarah's dad took us. Oh, and the one night out with the girls from the eight." She nodded toward the restaurant block. "Do you know there's even a Panda Express over there?"

"You're joking."

"Nope." Cass pointed past the restaurants to the edge of the official Olympic area. "See over there? Laura and I were at that little park the other day and on the way back we decided to grab some dinner. Since the food place was closer than the residential area, we stopped in. You wouldn't believe it, Coach. Baja, Panda, there's even a Tommy's!"

Sheila said nothing, just raised an eyebrow. It went without saying that eating that sort of food, even on a day off, would not help you stay in condition.

Cass laughed. "No worries, Coach. It was all fast food, so we just came back here. Laura said you'd make us do extra circuits at the gym if you caught us eating junk!"

"I'm not *that* bad. You know what you can and can't do to remain effective. However, I am not above the occasional 'I told you so' when it's warranted." Her dark eyes studied Cass a moment, her expression curious. "So. You and Laura have become friends?"

Cass shuffled her feet and looked down. She turned away from the city, swinging her legs around and then standing to rest her butt against the wall. "Yes," she said finally, slowly, as if still thinking about it. "We're friends. At least, I think so. Sometimes..." Cass turned to face her coach, her eyes troubled. "We have these moments. You know? When we're talking and we get really close and it feels...I don't know. Great. Then, she just closes off. I can never tell if it's something I said, or did, or... It's frustrating."

Sheila was silent as Cass turned around again, bending and resting her arms on the low wall, her chin resting on one fist. She sighed and drained her water bottle while Cass waited for her response. She leaned forward and mirrored Cass's pose on the wall. "I'm pretty sure it's not you, Cass. Or, if it is, it's not *you*, but something, some*one* you remind her of."

"What do you mean?"

Sheila hesitated, then said quietly, "It's not my story to tell. If you want to know, you'll have to ask her."

"I will."

"I'll just ask one thing, okay?"

"Sure."

"I trust that you know this, but I need to say it." Sheila waited until Cass turned to face her. "Don't ask her until after tomorrow's time trials, okay?" She straightened up, stretching again. "I'm asking not just as her coach, knowing she's got an important event tomorrow. I'm asking as a friend of hers. There's a lot there, and it would be hard for her to put it aside and then race."

"Got it."

"Thanks."

Cass turned away again to lean on the wall, this time turning her eyes in the direction of the boathouses. Sheila followed her gaze, both looking toward a venue they had no hope of seeing from this distance. As the afternoon sun faded into the painted sky of early evening, Sheila considered the woman beside her. There was a lot to Cass Flynn, and, despite the upset to the team and ripples losing a team member had caused, Sheila was glad of the accident that had brought Cass to them now. She was good for them, Sheila realized. Good for the double scull team and good for the squad. And perhaps for one of them, more than just good.

CHAPTER TWENTY-TWO

The soft breeze did little to ease the sweltering heat still oppressing the village, but Cass turned her face toward it anyway. Eyes closed, she listened to the sounds of the city below her; muffled now in the deepest, stillest part of the night, that hour or so between darkness and dawn, when it seems the whole world is fast asleep. From the distant waterfront, Cass could faintly hear the soft chiming of the bells on the bows of the local boats as they danced in the harbor, teased by the incoming tide.

In the stillness, she reflected on yesterday's events. The traffic on the water had been increasing in the marina area, so much so that the Olympic committee had had to ask the Chinese security forces to increase the safety zone for the rowers as they practiced. Yesterday's time trials had been cut short when an overzealous camera crew had strayed too close to the racing lanes and swamped one of the Chinese singles as they neared the finish. Luckily, nobody had been injured, but the complaints from the teams had been enough to galvanize the committee into action. Finally.

Restless and on edge about her own heats coming in the morning, Cass had tossed and turned before finally creeping past her sleeping teammates and up to the roof of the building, looking for relief from the omnipresent heat, and for a little solitude. It had been hard to find any time alone since the entire squad had moved into the common room of their floor. The air conditioning in their individual rooms was still out and looked to remain so for the duration.

While she'd enjoyed the enforced togetherness as a chance to really bond with her teammates, especially Laura, Cass was looking for a little quiet time. She was solitary by nature and the constant company and forced closeness was an additional strain. She had not heard anyone stir as she made her careful way through the maze of mattresses on the floor, so she was surprised now to hear soft footfalls behind her. Turning, she saw Laura's distinctive figure emerge from the darkness. Cass smiled softly and whispered, "Hi."

"Hi back." Laura glanced around, squinting in the pre-dawn darkness. "Why are we whispering, is there anyone else up here?"

"'Cause it's really quiet and no, nobody's up here, just me. And you."

"Yeah, I saw you leave and when you didn't come back, I... well, I was worried." Laura stepped closer, her eyes on Cass's face. "Everything okay?"

"Yeah." Cass smiled into Laura's eyes, enjoying the current of excitement she felt when Laura was near. Her fingers itched to reach out, to touch the strong face in front of her, but she stilled them, afraid of losing the tenuous connection they had now, of being rejected. Cass broke away from Laura's gaze, turning to catch the slight breeze again. "I, um, couldn't sleep."

Laura moved next to her, leaning her butt against the low rooftop wall. Her shoulder brushed Cass's as they stared in opposite directions into the night. "Nerves? Or the heat?"

"No. Yes. Both, I guess."

"You'll be great, I know it." Laura gently bumped Cass's shoulder. "Your times the last two weeks were amazing, weren't they?" Laura waited a moment. "Coach was actually smiling after the heats, so you know she's excited. You two set new personal bests yesterday, despite the chaos on the water. My boat's started calling yours the 'little engine that could,' you know."

"I know. Just, well, nerves. You get them too, don't you?" Without waiting for Laura's response, Cass continued, "I want us to do well. All of us."

"You *will* be great, you know," Laura repeated her earlier assurance. "I only hope our eight goes as well tomorrow."

"Oh, no fear of that. You all tore up the course in practice. You'll win, I'm sure of it." Cass lifted her eyes to meet Laura's gaze in the darkness. It was easier here, in the dark, just to look at her friend. She did not have to hide how she felt in the dark and was not worried that Laura would see too much. Laura had opened up a lot in the last two weeks and they were on the way to being good friends, despite the taller woman's tendency to pull back from anything too personal. Anyone who got *too* close. Every time Cass tried to get Laura to talk about herself the walls came up again. It seemed like for every step forward there was one back. It was frustrating, but everything in her told her that it was worth it to take those steps with Laura.

Cass replayed the coach's words, turning them over and over in her mind. *It's not my story to tell, you'll have to ask her.* Was it worth the risk of their friendship, she wondered? She was intrigued, by Laura and by how she felt when they were together. Or apart. Laura's face, or her eyes, or her smile, would pop up in her mind when she least expected it. Each time sending that tingling feeling straight to her stomach. Was it worth it? Yes, Cass thought. It was. *She* was.

"Thanks." Laura nudged Cass with her shoulder. "Don't overthink this stuff, Cass. You'll psych yourself right out of the regatta."

Cass sighed softly. "I just…" She paused. "I want it so *much*, though, you know?"

"I do." Something in Laura's voice pulled at Cass, made her

ache just a little, as Laura continued. "It's hard, isn't it? Wanting something so much, almost *too* much, knowing that one small thing could keep it from you."

Cass wondered if Laura were still talking about the upcoming races. She hoped not. She didn't want to read too much into their time together that day at the park, or into the brief conversations they'd had since. While she wasn't at all sure how Laura felt about her, Cass knew how she, herself, felt and was afraid of it. It was not logical to feel for somebody what she felt for Laura this fast, especially in this situation. *It's the emotion of the Olympics, the excitement. It's just you. She hasn't hinted either way...* "Laura?" Cass suddenly heard herself speaking and started in surprise. She hadn't meant to speak at all.

"Yeah?" Laura's soft voice was silken in the night and sent a shiver down Cass's spine.

"I...um..." *Oh shit! Nice, chicken, now what?* "I'm really glad you...I mean, that we started over. That we've become friends. It means a lot to me." Cass trailed off, sure her blush was lighting up the roof like a beacon.

Laura shifted and Cass felt Laura's fingers slide down her arm to tangle with her own. Laura's bigger, calloused hand enveloped hers and Cass felt the warmth of her touch spread from her hand to encompass her body. Laura gently squeezed once before letting go and easing Cass into a hug. "So am I, Cass. So am I."

Cass settled against the solid warmth of Laura's body. Forgetting the still, humid heat of the night and her nervousness about the upcoming races, she just let herself slide deeper into the embrace. It felt like coming home. She fit here, tucked into Laura's arms, against the steady beat of Laura's heart. Here she was safe and the woman holding her...solid. Laura's hands tightened against her back and pulled her even closer. Cass let out a sigh and wrapped her arms around Laura's solid strength. *This is good. This...I could get used to. Guess I do have a hint as to how she feels.*

"So, have you thought of your question yet?"

"Hmm?" Cass burrowed in a bit deeper into the hug trying to figure out what question Laura was talking about. Their quiet moment in the park a few days earlier popped into her thoughts and she considered briefly before answering, “Yup, but not now, okay?” she asked, mindful of her promise to their coach.

“Mmh.”

How long they stood there, Cass had no idea. Eventually, she felt Laura lift her head from where it lay resting atop her own and gently release her. Laura slid her hands down along Cass’s arms, then pushed off the wall and tugged Cass toward to rooftop door.

“C’mon, sport. Let’s get some sleep. Plenty of time for hugging after you win next week.”

In the darkness, Cass smiled and enjoyed the warmth of her hand held in Laura’s. “Yes, Coach.” She squeezed the hand holding hers once more.

“Besides,” Cass added, “you need your rest more than I do. You have a race to win tomorrow.”

Hands clasped loosely together, they left the dark stillness of the city behind them.

CHAPTER TWENTY-THREE

The water rippled softly, indicating the tiny bit of wind across the course. It was enough to cool but not enough to impede the racers, and Cass hoped it stayed that way for the race. Though she couldn't see it, she knew what was happening at the start. The team in the eight, ready to go, Amy asking them to count off, then telling them to hold steady. Behind Amy, at the stern, would be the volunteer's hands, preventing the sleek scull from drifting away from the start. The race director would be checking the teams off while Amy was performing one last check of her crew and craft. Cass had never rowed a cox'd boat, a boat directed by a coxswain, but she knew the procedure. Amy would be running through her own mental checklist, calling out the seat number of each woman and nodding sharply to their "ready" response. The rate counter on the cox-box would be set and ready, and Amy would make one left and right push with her feet to clear the tiny rudder one last time. Then she'd settle in, her eyes on the boat's leader, the stroke. On Laura.

The crowd around her shifted, allowing Cass and her group access to the rail that circled the runoff area. The move also now gave Cass an unimpeded view of the giant big screen positioned at the end of the course, and Cass sucked in a sharp breath as she looked up at the giant screen. As if the camera crew had read her thoughts, there, larger than life, was a close-up of Laura's tight, focused features. She couldn't hear what Laura said, but Cass saw her lips move in response to something, probably Amy's check. Even on the pixilated screen, the intensity of Laura's green eyes shined through and her gaze flicked up once, directly into the camera. Directly into Cass. Cass felt her heart stutter for a second before beating faster than before. She wiped suddenly sweaty palms on her shorts and took a steadying breath.

The camera's focus pulled back, giving them all a clear view of the start line. Lined up precisely at the start, bright white numbers mounted on the bow just behind the bow ball, the boats sat sleek and ready. The quivers of the boats as the crews moved gave the illusion that the sculls were eager to race. Cass's eyes stayed on Laura's boat, and she watched as Laura rolled her shoulders in her familiar pattern—once forward, once back, and once more forward—before settling her oar gently back in the water, causing barely a ripple in the glass-like surface.

Volunteers lay along the end of the starting docks, forearms hanging down, hands gently cradling the aft deck and holding the boats in place. Their job was to prevent any drift that might give a team an advantage or cause a false start.

The faint commands of the starter could be heard over the incessant chatter of the announcers' voices coming from the huge speakers near the stands. "Ready all crews," was followed by the roll call of the lanes. When the announcer said, "Lane number three, the United States," Amy's response at the start was drowned out by the noise of her teammates on this end of the course cheering loudly, but Cass watched as Amy's hand rose in response.

Cass was concentrating intently on the images on the

screen, to the exclusion of everything else around her. The camera, which had been zoomed tightly in on the faces of the Chinese crew, suddenly moved with dizzying speed to focus on the U.S. boat. The look of fierce concentration on Laura's face was simply breathtaking, and Cass found herself mesmerized as she gazed into the larger-than-life features. Once again Laura's gaze flickered up from where it was fixed on Amy's, up to the camera, and Cass again felt the power of those green eyes shoot through her. It felt for a second as if Laura had looked up at *her*, directly into her eyes. In the next instant, Laura's gaze was back on Amy's face, her focus complete.

Cass shook her head and then jumped as a buzzer sounded. It echoed the one at the start and she watched as suddenly all boats were away, each crew digging in for the power ten, ten hard and fast strokes at the start to establish position. Cass hated watching the camera coverage, because the forced perspective always looked skewed. She wished they'd just do aerial shots.

The boats surged forward, bobbing in and out of the water as the teams settled into their rhythms, lifting up as the women pulled powerfully through the water and settling again as they finished their stroke sequence. Up and down, up and down, Amy bobbing along at the back, a bright red speck tucked into the stern. The U.S. boat quickly flashed past the first buoy-marker and Cass glanced at the lap timer, then blinked. Wow. She was pretty certain this event would set a new course record.

As the chase boats, referees and camera boats jockeyed for position around the back end of the course, Cass kept one eye on the giant screen and another on the coach. The benefit of having a cox'd boat was that the coach heard what the rowers in the U.S. boat did. Amy's cox-box also offered a one-way broadcast on a specific channel and coach's headset was tuned to that channel. So were a set of referees, just to make sure the units hadn't been modified to receive signals from any coach. Or anyone else.

She saw Coach nod in satisfaction when the eight surged forward from the start, then, ten strokes in, settle into the rhythm they'd practiced. Tuning out the cheers and encouraging shouts echoing from the stands, Cass bent all of her focus to the slim blue craft she could now just make out in the distance. God, from this end it looked like an impossibly long course! The U.S. eight was running straight and true, positioned precisely in the center of the lane. From what she could see on the screen, it looked as if the women were in perfect sync. For a single instant she felt herself swept up again in the simple beauty of her sport. It was so often easy to lose sight of what had drawn her to the sport in the first place; the elegant lines of the scull, the swinging sweep of the oars, the sleek knife-edged cut the craft made through the water. That often got lost in the *work* of the sport.

The noise of the crowd around her sharply drew Cass's focus back. The Chinese were going wild. The top two finishers of this race would go on to the medal round, and the long red Chinese eight was surging forward as the sculls neared the halfway mark. Even from the odd warped perspective of the camera crews racing alongside the crews, Cass could see that this challenge from China would be difficult to fend off. She glanced at Coach's face and was surprised by the look of...what? Fear? Anger? Something wasn't right. Cass leaned close to her and asked, "What's wrong, Coach?"

Sheila shook her head, her expression tight, her eyes on the women just now coming into focus on this end of the course. Her voice tight, tense, she answered, "Not sure. Amy's giving more directional commands. Not just stroke counts." The coach's words were choppy, her attention on the tiny blue speck that was the U.S. eight craft. Suddenly she shook her head and uttered, "Damn it!"

Cass looked from her to the giant screen and felt her heart drop. The U.S. boat was off-center in the lane, just slightly off course. What the hell was happening on the water? Just as quickly as they'd moved off center they were back on again, and Cass saw them correct again. *Saw* them.

Saw the *port* side dig a bit deeper to correct.

Saw the *starboard* side pull again to correct.

Oh crap.

Cass looked again to Sheila's face and suddenly understood. Amy had no rudder control! Without the rudder to steer their course, she had to rely solely on the arm strength and evenness of the crew's strokes. She couldn't make any adjustments, couldn't keep them true. That meant extra work for her and for the women pulling the boat forward with every stroke.

Once again the long blue craft drifted off-center and once again Amy's sharp command to the women in her boat fixed the problem. Cass suddenly wondered if the broken rudder were slowing the boat down.

As if she'd said it out loud, Sheila muttered, "Something's wrong with that boat." She leaned to her right and waved an assistant over. "Make sure you have a video camera on that boat from now on until I tell you to stop!" The assistant nodded as Sheila continued. "Keep the focus on Amy and try to catch any movement by the rudder cable." Again the assistant nodded. Sheila turned to Cass. "I'm going to grab an official, I want this lodged immediately." She took two steps away then swore softly, turning back to Cass. Ripping the headphones off of her head she slapped them into Cass's hands. "Listen! Call my cell if anything...*more*...happens."

Stunned, Cass could only nod. She fumbled with the headset and finally got it settled onto her head in time to hear Amy's sharp command, "Power ten in two, ready? One. *Two*!" Cass watched the U.S. boat surge forward again with the new effort. Now she had a steady running commentary in her ear, that single voice drowning out the voices around her.

"Steady, girls! Steady! Two more to go, keep it up, you've got it! Pull! Port side, easy two, now steady on. Good rhythm. We're on the way, girls! Keep steady, don't slip! Six! Watch your angle. Less of the splash, everyone! Fifteen-hundred to go. We pull again in ten, I'll count them for you. And ten, nine, eight, seven, six, five, four, power ten in two and ready? One, two! Hard on it, girls! Hard! Pull hard! Pull!"

Cass had to remind herself to breathe as she listened, her eyes glued to the boats hurtling down the course toward them. She flicked her gaze back and forth between the image on the screen and the boats slicing through the calm water. The crowd noise was overwhelming as once again the overhead camera focused on the sleek red Chinese boat charging forward. But, as the red boat moved, so too did the white Swiss scull, the women determined not to be left out of the race. Again the U.S. boat slipped slightly off of the centerline of the lane, this time to port, and Amy's sharp correction blasted through the headset, mixed seamlessly with her commands.

"One thousand to go! Starb'd! Steady-on, watch your position! Port, push on! All crew, drive hard, pull hard! You've got this, you have to do it, you have to pull. This is our *time,* our *race! Nobody takes that from us! Five and six, put your backs into it! Stepping up the rate in two. Ready? One, two! Up two, ladies, up two! It's time, let's roll! Counting down to the last power ten in five, and...five, four, three... ready? One, two!"*

If Amy's voice had been sharp before, now it was piercing in Cass's ear. She could hear an echo of it out on the water, too. Amy's voice drowning in a sea of other coxswains' yells, and all overpowered by the shouts and screams of the fans. Where before they had seemed to crawl to the finish, now they were flying down the lanes. Amy had them on true now and they were surging forward with the other boats.

The crowd went wild as the boats streaked past the stands, the camera and officials' launches in their wake. Past the far end of the stands, past the midline, with the high announcer's booth, past the near end of the stands, lifting out of the water with each stroke, flying down to the finish buoys.

In her ear, Cass heard Amy scream, "*Race five, race five, go! Five! Four! Three! Two! One!*" Each count was in time to a stroke, each one coming faster upon the last as Amy increased the stroke speed. This was the racing stroke the team used in the last seconds to propel themselves forward. The slim blue hull surged forward with each pull and now the crews were close enough for Cass to hear the other cox's yells responding to Amy's call for a final push. The blasts of the finish horn signaled the end of the race, but Cass wasn't sure who'd placed and where. She jumped up, trying to see, pulling off the headset in the process. As she strained, a hand came down on her shoulder.

"They're out," said Sheila grimly. "Missed the top two by a stroke, it looks like, but I've filed an official inquiry."

"What?" Cass couldn't believe it. "Out?" You're—" But she stopped, arrested by the look on the coach's face. No, she wasn't kidding at all.

Sheila turned to the assistant standing nearby, her camera

still focused on the now drifting U.S. eight-boat, its rowers collapsed over one another in exhaustion, chests heaving as they sucked in much-needed oxygen. "Get down to the put-in, make sure nobody touches the end of that scull. Keep your camera on it from the second it comes out of the water until I can get there with the officials."

"Got it," said Karen, nodding sharply. She turned and sprinted toward the put-in, where the boats would be coming out of the water.

"Cass, get down there too and let Amy know what's going on. I want Laura to keep the team close. Again, don't let anyone near the end of that boat!" Cass echoed Karen's nod and took off. She threaded her way through the throng as the announcement came, blaring the results for the crowd.

"The results, ladies and gentlemen, of the semifinal heat. Switzerland, first. China, second, the United States, third, Canada, fourth and Great Britain, fifth. These results mean that Switzerland and China are guaranteed slots in the final in three days time. The remaining three crews will compete in the repechage, the second-chance race, tomorrow. The winner of that race will move on to the final 'A' round."

The announcer's voice was drowned out by the shouts of the crowd, some happy, some angry. Cass could see the disappointment on the faces of the women in the U.S. eight as she got to the dock. Some were shaking their heads and Ellie was comforting Jan who'd burst into tears at the news. She nodded to Karen, the assistant coach with the camera. "I'll let them know." But before she could say anything to her teammates, Amy's angry voice carried over the water.

"Karen! Call Coach down here. We've got—"

Cass waved her hand and called back. "We know. Coach is on it. Keep everyone clear of the rudder as you come in." She waited for Amy's nod before looking over at Laura's face. Set and angry, even from this distance Cass could see her bright green eyes blazing with frustration and barely suppressed fury. She caught Laura's gaze and offered her a small, encouraging smile, hoping to convey somehow that she understood. That she knew what it was like to be standing on the edge and then to have the world yanked out from under your feet.

Oh yeah, Cass knew it well.

This time, however, she didn't have to just take it. This time there was something to fight. As the boat glided to a controlled stop at the edge of the dock, Cass reached up to help the first rower out. One by one the women stepped out, careful to keep the end of the scull clear of the dock. Cass glanced once up at Karen, happy to see her still focusing on the stern of the boat. She turned back and reached a hand in to help Laura out.

"I can do it," Laura muttered, her teeth clenched in anger.

Cass blew out a frustrated breath. "Laura, let me help." She held her hand out again, glancing once at Amy and then locking her gaze on Laura's face. She said nothing else, just kept her hand out there, hoping Laura would reach out. Would take it. Would accept what she was offering.

Laura's green-eyed gaze was cold and sharp as she flicked her eyes from Cass's face to her hand, then back again. Slowly her eyes warmed, her jaw loosened. She took a long, steadying breath, then reached out to grasp Cass's hand in hers. As Cass pulled her out of the boat, Laura gave the fingers tangled with hers a quick squeeze. "Thanks," she whispered as she steadied herself on the dock.

Cass squeezed back once before releasing Laura's hand. "Any time," she answered with a gentle smile.

Another step forward.

CHAPTER TWENTY-FOUR

The soft moan and rustle of cotton woke Cass. It took her a moment to place the noise—she'd been deeply asleep. Most nights, she dropped into an exhausted slumber the minute her head hit the pillow, and last night had been the exception. The qualifying heat for Laura's event had been the most exciting racing Cass had ever seen and, despite the exhaustion of her own workouts, she'd had a hard time shutting her brain down after the thrilling finish of the trial. Not to mention the chaos that followed when the officials found not one problem with the U.S. eight, but two. Severed cables. Neatly cut almost all the way through. Damaged enough that with the slightest pressure they would give way, just as they had

Whoever had done it had known just what they were doing. They had also been so intent on damaging the U.S. women's chances that they'd gone too far. The officials might have chalked one snapped cable up to chance, but two was damning. Someone had tampered with the U.S. boat. Sabotage.

Coach had been livid and, after a heated discussion with the officials on the docks and a meeting later between the teams involved in the heat, had demanded that the U.S. eight be advanced to the final without having to race the repechage. The officials had waffled, and in the end had ignored the demands of not only Coach Adler, but the other coaches. It was unprecedented, but the Chinese were determined to preserve the honor of the event, and not to lose face on the international racing scene. The eight would race the repechage, the "second chance" race for a shot at a place in the final "A" group, the medal round.

Exhausted body and overstimulated brain did not a good combination make. Laura's crew had done extremely well despite the sabotage of their boat, coming in a very close third. Their strong finish left no doubt as to what the results would have been had their boat not been tampered with. Despite their strong performance, the fact that they had to race the repechage had brought them down and the squad was subdued as they cleaned up and returned to the dorms. Nobody wanted to advance this way.

Cass yawned and wondered who was on duty near the boats tonight. Coach had worked out a schedule of rotating "watch" teams in light of today's events, pulling from the assistants and some of the parents. For a moment, Cass allowed herself to picture Big John Sullivan coming face-to-face with their would-be saboteur, then she shook her head. She really didn't want to think of what he might do.

The clock at the end of the room chimed, and Cass found herself blinking sleepily into the darkness, trying to pinpoint what had awakened her. The room was dark, the faint light that sneaked through the blinds casting soft shadows around the room. Around her, the mumbles and sleeping noises of her twenty-two roommates blended into the quiet of the night. *You're imagining things, Cass. Just go back to...*

This time the moan was accompanied by a faint whimper and Cass quickly turned to see Laura, her face kissed by the dim light, moving restlessly on her mattress. Cass leaned closer, surprised to see a faint sheen of sweat covering Laura's face. Laura tossed her head from side to side, her face frozen into a grimace.

Oh crap. Is she sick? Nightmare? I don't want to wake her, but she's getting louder.

Slowly, Cass reached out, gently resting her hand on Laura's arm, hoping to calm her friend. She was as startled as Laura when Laura slapped her hand away and sat up with a start.

"No! I–"

"Shh, Laura, shh." Cass kept her voice low, soothing, despite the pounding of her heart. *What the* hell *was that?*

"I...Cass?" Laura glanced around, then lowered her voice. "What's going on?"

"You were...are you okay? Are you sick or something?"

Laura slowly settled back onto her mattress, lying on her side and facing Cass. She wiped her hand across her forehead, frowning at the dampness that came away. She took her sheet and wiped her face and neck before reaching for her bottle of water. Downing most of it in a few swallows, she closed her eyes.

Cass rolled onto her back, unconsciously rubbing the hand that Laura had slapped. Her heart rate was getting back to normal, and she let out a long, slow breath. Whatever was going on, she didn't think Laura was sick. She turned back onto her side and faced her friend. With their mattresses side-by-side, their faces were only inches apart.

"Laura?" Cass whispered, not wanting to wake anyone else.

"Yeah."

"You okay?"

"Um yeah, I guess so. Thanks for waking me. I, um, I get them sometimes. The nightmares."

"Want to talk about it?"

Laura waited a long moment before she opened her eyes and quirked a small, tired smile at Cass. "Does this count as your question?"

Cass shifted and propped one arm under the side of her head, then dropped the other to rest on the edge of her mattress, her fingers idly playing with the part of Laura's sheet that overlapped her own. She studied what she could see of Laura's face in the dark, able to make out only vague outlines. Despite being on two mattresses in a crowded room, this felt almost...intimate. Everyone around her was sleeping—even most of the village outside their dorm was asleep. She was close enough that she could smell Laura's shampoo, sort of salty-sweet in the pervasive moist air that hung in the room. Laura's breath mingled with her own as she settled more comfortably. Cass waited, giving Laura time to recover. Finally she answered Laura's question, "Yeah, it counts."

Laura sighed and rolled onto her back, laying one arm over her eyes. She lifted her other hand up, almost beseechingly, then let it fall against the mattress. Her fingers curled into a fist.

Cass said nothing. After a minute she bit her lip and reached out to close her hand over Laura's fist. She gave the tense fingers a brief squeeze and waited.

Slowly, Laura relaxed her hand and turned her palm up, tangling her fingers with Cass's. She spoke in a low voice, careful not to break the spell, the silence of the night.

"It always starts the same. I'm at home. Studying, actually. I am prepping for my boards. My phone rings." Laura lifted the arm across her eyes slightly and turned her head toward Cass. "I was in the last year of my grad program in psych. Sports psych, to be precise. Anyway, my clinicals were done and my boards were scheduled for the next day. My phone rings and—"

Cass squeezed the tense fingers wrapped in her own. The pain in Laura's voice was achingly hard to hear.

Laura cleared her throat softly and then stumbled on. "When I got there, the cops were already there. I had to fight and push my way in. I came around the corner...to the bedroom. The bathroom...oh God. Shelly, my girlfriend, was there, holding Bren. Bren was..." Laura choked back a sob. "Bren, beautiful, fun Bren. She had...cut...herself. Slit...h-h-her—"

"Shh, it's okay, Laura, it's okay. You're not there. You're here. Shh. It's all right." *God! No it's not all right! Holy shit! Poor Laura. Poor Bren.* "Laura? Who was Bren?"

"Brenda, actually. She is—was—Shelly's sister."

"Oh, God. I'm sorry."

The hand in Cass's was trembling, and Laura wiped tears from her face with her other arm. She turned her face to Cass, a pleading expression on her face.

"I tried. God, I tried. I told them. Told her I wasn't qualified to help Brenda. Told her that she needed help, *real* help. That I couldn't do it." Laura sobbed softly, her eyes begging Cass to understand. "Honest to God, Shelly, I tried," she pleaded.

Cass gathered Laura into her arms, knowing that at that moment, Laura wasn't seeing her, but someone else...Shelly. "Shh, Laura. Shh. It's okay. It's not your fault, it's okay." Over and over she murmured reassurances, rocking Laura gently, feeling her tears soak into her shirt. Slowly Laura's tears stopped and Cass reluctantly let her go. Laura's broken whisper was harsh in the darkness.

"Shelly blamed me. She, I don't know. She swore I never told Bren to see a real counselor. She insisted to the police, to everyone, that I'd demanded to see Bren, that I'd forced her to talk to me." Laura closed her eyes and covered them again with her arm. She reached blindly for Cass's hand again. "I swear to God I didn't. I was cocky, but I also knew what I couldn't do. Bren had issues. Issues that Shelly wouldn't face. Still won't face. They both have...had...them."

"When did...when did this happen? How long ago?" *How long have you been carrying this?*

"It was a year on July second."

The day after I got here. No wonder she was...Christ. What an anniversary. Cass said nothing. She lay there, her hand in Laura's, trying to offer what comfort she could. "You still feel guilty." Laura turned to face Cass, staring intently at their joined hands. Her thumb ran over Cass's knuckles, back and forth, in a seemingly unconscious gesture of comfort. For whom, Cass wasn't sure.

"Yeah."

"You know, though, there's nothing you could have done, right?"

"Yeah."

Cass tugged on Laura's hand and waited until Laura looked at her. In the darkness, she could only see the faint shimmer of

Laura's eyes and the soft curve of her cheekbone. She could feel Laura's eyes on her own.

"I mean it, Laura. It. Was. Not. Your. Fault." She emphasized each word with a gentle shake of their joined hands.

They lay there, silently, staring at one another in the darkness. Cass felt more than saw Laura's nod and was content with that. For now. She shifted and stuffed her pillow under her head, keeping her other hand where it was. She reveled in the warmth of Laura's fingers tangled with her own and hoped she had given her friend some comfort.

Slowly Laura's breathing evened out and she slept as Cass kept watch against more bad dreams.

CHAPTER TWENTY-FIVE

Laughter echoed across the water as Laura and Cass guided the team's practice single rowing shells back to the dock. The two carried on the friendly bickering they'd been doing since they had signed the boats out earlier, trading mock jibes across the water; Cass teasing Laura about her inability to manage two oars at a time while Laura returned fire with some well-placed pokes of her own. The final race had been for a prize and Cass began mentally listing the options for dinner, since Laura now owed Cass after that last race.

Cass easily lifted the shells out of the water while Laura dried the oars. Two other squad members were signed up to use the boats, so they didn't have to bring them inside. As Cass rose, Laura slung a companionable hand over her shoulder and spun her around. Cass glanced up at Laura's laughing face and grinned back, feeling considerably lighter than she had in days.

The gate at the top of the dock clanged as someone entered and she looked up automatically. Squinting against the bright sunlight, Cass studied the approaching woman and was surprised when she felt Laura suddenly stiffen beside her. Laura slowly dropped her arm from Cass's shoulder and took a deliberate step forward, putting space between them and placing Cass slightly behind her.

Tan and golden and backlit by the afternoon sun, the woman was stepping gingerly from the shore to the floating pier, carefully stepping around coiled line and the detritus of scattered rigging and gear. Cass watched as she stopped and spoke with the guard at the gate, flashed her ID badge, then patted him on the shoulder condescendingly as she passed. The newcomer's eyes locked with Laura's as she approached, then slid downward to study Cass, leaving her feeling slightly...soiled. The smug smile the newcomer had been wearing disappeared and her eyes narrowed slightly.

Laura must have seen the change in expression because she quickly stepped forward, her voice sharper and more bitter than Cass had ever heard it. "What are you doing here, Shelly?"

"I'm here officially. The network wanted some stringers on the stories. Angie knew I competed in college, so..." Shelly shrugged. "Here I am."

Running a hand through her hair, Laura stood as if frozen.

From behind her, Cass studied the woman, trying to figure out what was going on. The lightness of the early afternoon was gone, replaced with a tension she could feel radiating off Laura and hostility from the woman before them. Tall, taller than Laura even, her sun-kissed skin and straight blond hair, her crisp white cotton shirt with the logo of her television network embroidered above the left breast pocket, her perfectly creased white shorts, and her long, softly muscled legs completed the picture of sport-chic that some women could carry off with panache. Cass shifted the oars in her hands, suddenly acutely aware of her damp workout unitard, wind-tangled hair and bare feet.

"Cass, this is Michelle. Shelly is my, uh..."

"Girlfriend." Shelly arched a perfectly shaped blond brow at Laura. "I believe that's the word you're looking for."

"Oh. I..." *Oh shit.* Uneasily, Cass took a step back. *This isn't happening. I did not fall in lo— This is not happening.* Suddenly nauseous, Cass was very aware that they hadn't talked about Shelly the night Laura had opened up. She'd just assumed that Laura's girlfriend had dumped her. Assumed that...that there was nothing there, but... *I can't imagine staying with someone who blames you for the death of their sister. Girlfriend. Crap. Oh man, I've messed up here.* Cass shifted her equipment again, looking for someone to help Laura get their gear up to the boat house. She needed to get out of here, fast.

"I'd shake your hand, but..." Cass shrugged, juggling the oars and her shoes, trying to keep her gym bag on her shoulder.

"That's fine, no need. Really." Dismissing Cass with a sniff, Shelly turned her attention to Laura.

Shaking her head slightly, Cass muttered, "It's nice to meet you." Barely able to look at Laura, Cass shouldered her way past.

"*Ex*-girlfriend." Laura glared at Shelly a moment before reaching out to catch Cass's shoulder. "Ex, Cass. *Ex*. I don't want you to think...I mean, we, you and I—"

"Look, it's okay," she said. "We're friends, right? So, no explanations necessary. Go on, she came a long way to see you. I've got to get this stuff washed down. I'll tell Artie we're back so the others can use the, um, shells. And, ah, so you can..." Cass trailed off, aware that she was babbling. Shaking off Laura's hand, Cass quickly left the dock but remained within earshot, missing the flash of pain that crossed Laura's face.

Spinning around, Laura gripped Shelly's elbow. "What the *hell* is this about? You're not my *girlfriend*! You dumped *me*, remember?"

"Oh, sorry. Am I ruining something?" Shelly tossed her hair back, giving Laura a saccharine smile. "I'm *ever* so sorry to have ruined your day."

"What do you want, Shel?"

"Oh, come on Laura, I thought it was funny." Shelly lifted her sunglasses, her blue eyes hard as ice chips as she stared at

Laura. "It was funny, you and I. Funny right up until you killed my baby sister."

Cass clenched her fists. She kept her face turned slightly away and tried to focus on what she was doing, fighting the urge to jump up and pull Laura away. To get them both out of here. Everything in her screamed to go back, but this, she realized, was none of her business.

Laura shuddered again and squeezed her eyes shut, clenching her fists as she fought for control. Then she glared at Shelly, her green eyes blazing in the evening light. "I did not kill Brenda, Shel. She killed herself."

"No. I don't think so."

"What the hell do you mean?"

"You may not have been the one to put the razor to her wrists, but you sure as hell helped her along."

"Shel. Shelly, I—" Laura swallowed, hard, her face paling slightly. "God, Shel. I tried everything I knew. I *told* her, I told *you* that I was not qualified. That she needed to see someone better, someone more experienced. I—"

"No. This was not Brenda's fault and it's certainly not mine. You, Laura. It's all on you. And someday, you'll get what you deserve. And, if there is a God, I'll be there to see it happen." Shelly spun quickly and strode up the dock, pushing aside several rowers returning from their workout, leaving Laura shaking in her wake.

Cass stayed where she was, her back to the dock gate, as Shelly blew past. She doubted the woman even noticed she was still there.

Laura slowly sank down to her knees, her every movement slow, painful to see. She slipped her feet over the side and into the water, resting her head in her hands, her shoulders shaking slightly.

Cass went to her. Whatever she thought they'd had, whatever it was that Shelly thought she and Laura still had, Laura was still a friend. A friend in so much pain that it pulled at Cass, leaving an ache in her chest. She silently approached Laura, where she sat hunched on the edge of the dock and, hesitating briefly, laid a gentle hand upon her shoulder.

Laura's head jerked up at Cass's touch and when she turned to face her, her green eyes blazed bright and angry. It took everything she had not to recoil at the venom in Laura's gaze. The flash of fury was so brief that Cass wondered if she imagined it.

She opened her mouth to speak, but Laura shook her head. "Go," she said, in a tone that brooked no argument. "Leave me alone."

Laura sat and stared at the water, her eyes and thoughts far away, and Cass left her.

CHAPTER TWENTY-SIX

Coach Sheila Adler kicked her sneakers off and settled her stocking feet up on her desk. This was her quiet hour, the time after dinner. She wanted to review the team's upcoming time trial slots and take a quick look at the performance times of her crews. Overall, things were looking good, and she wanted to do what she could to keep it that way. A soft knock interrupted her thoughts.

"Hey, Coach, got a minute?"

"Sure, Cass. I told you to call me Sheila, remember? We're not so formal around here, you know. What's on your mind?"

Sheila waved Cass to one of the chairs in the tiny office she shared with her assistants. Cass gingerly sat, perched on the edge of the chair, looking as if she'd flee at the first sign of trouble.

After watching Cass fidget and shift for fully a minute, Sheila softly cleared her throat.

"So, is this a social call?"

"Uh, no. It's not a team thing either. Well, it *is*, sort of, but..." Cass thrust her fingers through her hair, disrupting the curls and sending them tumbling end over end. She abruptly stood and began to pace the small office. Two strides away, stop, turn, two strides back.

"I uh, well, the other night Laura had a nightmare. I mean, you know, we're all out in the common room and... Anyway, she had a really bad dream and told me...she told me. About Brenda, about the suicide, about Shelly blaming her."

"Okay."

"Fine. Okay. Well, we've, Laura and I, we've been getting along really well and..." Cass stopped again and stared at Sheila for a moment, a puzzled expression on her face. "I don't even know why I'm telling you this."

"Maybe you just need to talk, Cass. It's okay."

Cass took a deep breath and returned to her chair. "Okay. Today, this afternoon, we were at the docks. Messing around, you know? I challenged her to a race, so we borrowed the practice singles and, well, had a blast, really."

"So I heard." Sheila's tone was dry. She'd heard about the impromptu singles race from one of the assistants, who was chortling about Laura's poor showing. Sweep rowers made bad scullers, with no practice time to adapt. Personally, Sheila was delighted that Laura was willing to play; however, the coach side of her wasn't entirely sure how she felt about it. One thing was sure, though, she'd never seen her number one rower relax enough to simply have fun. That made for a nice change.

"Yeah, well, anyway. Someone...*Shelly*, showed up at the docks, and—"

"What?" The coach sat forward. This wasn't good news.

"Yeah. Shelly. She introduced herself as..." Cass swallowed hard, her face a pale shade of green. "Laura's *girlfriend*."

The office was silent as Sheila studied Cass's miserable face. It was obvious the younger woman was in pain and that bothered Sheila a great deal. Romances on a team always meant one of two things; either everything ran better than ever or everything went to hell. If Sheila wasn't careful, the team that had been moving along smoothly might soon be opening door number two. She watched Cass struggle for control while she thought things out. Obviously, Cass was in far deeper than her "getting along well" statement implied. She knew the two women were becoming close, but Cass looked more upset than a simple friend would normally be by the sudden appearance of an apparent girlfriend. Well, there was something she could do about *that*, at least.

"That's crap."

"Yeah, I know."

"No, Cass. What I mean is, Shelly is not Laura's girlfriend."

The relief on Cass's face was almost comical.

"No?" Cass backpedaled quickly. "I mean, I didn't *think* so and after the last few weeks...but it...I...I mean, she. Shelly. She was so...damn. She was so *confident*. You know?"

"I do know and the answer is still no. Laura told me that Shelly ordered Laura to get the hell out the night of Brenda's... well, the night Brenda died. As far as I know, Laura hasn't seen her since. Shelly even had Laura barred from the funeral."

"You're kidding."

"No, I'm not."

Cass collapsed weakly back into her chair, as if she couldn't help herself. "I knew it. I knew I couldn't fall...I mean, I didn't think Laura would..." Cass stood again, this time going to stand at the window. It was night and with the lights on in the office, the only thing visible in the window was her own reflection. She turned to face Sheila, her expression clear, her voice firmer now than it had been when she came in. "Thanks, Coach. I mean, thanks, Sheila. I guess you're the only person I could ask, you know?"

"Why didn't you ask Laura?"

"I think I was afraid of the answer."

"Understandable. Cass, look. This is an emotional time, and I don't just mean for you all. It is for everyone. The Olympics generate their own weather, if you will. Emotional weather. Don't get too caught up in it—" Sheila held up her hand before Cass protested. "Wait." Her voice was commanding, but still caring.

"Don't get too caught up in it, but don't close yourself away from the possibilities either. Trust me, I know from personal experience. Magical things can happen in this atmosphere, but for them to happen you have to put your fear aside."

Cass nodded thoughtfully, her eyes distant. After a moment she raised her head and Sheila was pleased to see the familiar grin back in place.

"Got it, Coach, and thanks."

"No worries." Checking her watch, Sheila decided that she'd call it quits early tonight. "Join me for some coffee at the café?"

"Can't. Gotta go find someone."

Sheila walked with Cass outside, then watched her athlete head back to the dorms. She had a feeling Laura wouldn't be able to run from this one. And that was a good thing.

CHAPTER TWENTY-SEVEN

"...as you know Bob, I have competed against some of these women and they simply are the best in the world."

"Very true Michelle. Very true. I understand you weren't too bad yourself, once upon a time. Can you give us any inside scoop on the U.S. team's chances this year?"

"Well, Bob, overall the team looks solid, although I have to say that it seems the coaching staff has made some questionable decisions this year."

"How so?"

"Well, first there was the addition of an older and, to be quite frank, somewhat less experienced athlete to replace the injured Gail Kennedy. Flynn is a bit past her prime, if you ask me. Rumor has it she's not even one hundred percent following the tragic accident of last year. Then, of course, there's Laura Kelley and her history well, it's all unproven of course, but—"

Amy hastily snapped off the radio, almost breaking the knob in her hurry to silence Shelly Michaels' spiteful voice. She looked around quickly, hoping everyone was too involved in their own workout routines to notice what the commentator had been saying. No such luck. Cass sat frozen on the low bench, weights dangling forgotten in her hands, her eyes locked on the floor at her feet. Across from her, Laura stood facing the mirror, her hands clenching and unclenching at her sides, her shoulders taut with anger. The rest of the team looked uncomfortable.

"Fucking bitch."

Laura's low rumble startled Amy. She stood and reached around Laura, pulling her hands free of the bar.

"Shh, pal, I know. She's a bitch. I don't know what you ever—I mean, I'm glad as hell that you're..." Amy stopped, obviously uncomfortable.

"No worries Ames. I know what you mean." Laura kept her back to the room as slowly activity began to pick up around them. "She's been at it like this all week. I wish to hell I could figure out her angle. She's bitching and sniping at all of us and, other than making herself look bad, I just don't get it."

"Yeah, I even heard the anchor from CBS say something about it the other day. I know Coach has about had it."

"Good." Laura shook out her hands and wrapped her fingers around the cold metal again, her grip so tight that her knuckles were white. She glanced in the mirror as a flash of auburn curls passed quickly by. Keeping her voice low, she asked Amy, "Did Cass hear?"

"Yeah."

"Fuck." Laura let the bar drop back into its rack, the loud clang startling Amy. "She doesn't need that, Amy. Is she okay?"

"Why don't you ask her yourself?"

"I can't. I—crap. I just can't, okay?" Laura grabbed her towel out of her bag and wiped her sweaty arms and face, her frustration and anger clear on her strong features. She lifted her face from the towel and pinned Amy with a piercing stare. "Make sure she's okay, will you Ames? I'm going to run a bit."

"Wait, Laura—" Amy's words were lost as Laura left the gym, her bag banging loudly against the door.

"God *damn* it!" The little cox's frustrated curse was lost in the thump and rumble of gym equipment.

CHAPTER TWENTY-EIGHT

"Thanks for the lift." Cass grabbed her duffel from the back of the English crew van and headed toward the boathouse. Giving the driver a final wave, she jogged down the path, around the corner of the building and along the waterfront, hoping to catch the team inside. She stopped just outside the cavernous space that housed the boats, appreciating, as she always did, the order and neatness of the place.

"Please, ma'am. Pass?"

The white-gloved security officer stepped forward, partially blocking Cass's entrance to the building. Cass wasn't certain what the little guard was there to prevent, she looked as if just about anyone could bulldoze past her. Smaller than Cass by nearly six inches, she was outgoing and friendly, and, Cass thought, about as threatening as a butterfly. She had haltingly told Cass earlier in the week that she loved to practice her English with anyone willing to cooperate and it was clear that she was simply enamored of all things American.

"Oh, yeah. Sure." Cass fished around under her T-shirt for the badge that hung around her neck. "How's it going, Yanmei?"

A smile blossomed on the young woman's face. She bowed slightly and waved Cass inside. "I am...well. Thank you," Yanmei said. "Please. Do you practice alone today?"

Cass raised her eyebrows and turned to face the guard fully. "Um, no." She glanced around, this time noting that all of her team's boats were secure in their racks. "Crap."

"I am sorry?"

"Oh. I'm sorry, Yanmei. That was rude. Uh, have you seen other members of my team? Team USA?"

"No. No, I do not see them today. It is only the English here and the Germany. No others are on my...plan?"

"Plan? Oh, your schedule. Great." Frustrated, Cass turned and left the boathouse, wondering what to do next and how she'd gotten her information so mixed up. She checked her watch—just short of ten in the morning. She was certain Sheila had said the team was heading over here after breakfast. She'd missed the team bus because she'd needed to have some ultrasound therapy done on her leg over at the clinic to relieve some cramping and now it looked like she was going to miss whatever the coach had planned for the day. Cass shaded her eyes with one hand as she studied the crews out on the water. *The Brits are still in mid warm-up. Germany? Maybe I can catch a ride back with them. Who the hell put the village thirty-five miles from the venue! It's probably the other way around, dummy. Crap. I don't want to ride back with—*

"Lose something?"

Shelly's brittle voice cut through Cass's thoughts, bringing other, more unwelcome things to mind. She knew the woman had deliberately misrepresented herself when they'd met on the dock the other day, and she was still mad at herself for giving Shelly the satisfaction of a reaction. She was sorry the woman had lost her sister, but to lay all of the blame at Laura's feet... *She certainly isn't here to get Laura back, at least not in the romantic sense.*

"No," she snapped back. "Have you? Oh, sorry, you can't lose what you've tossed away, can you?"

A neatly shaped eyebrow rose in the only reaction Shelly showed to Cass's comment. She dismissed Cass as quickly as she had the other day on the dock—unimportant, though worth trifling with if it suited her ultimate goal.

"Where's Laura?"

Cass shook her head. "Sorry, can't say."

"You *can't* say? Or you won't?"

"Can't, I'm afraid."

"Oh? Did she leave you behind, too?"

Taking a deep breath to control her already short temper, Cass silently counted to ten. "What do you want here?"

"What I want is for you to tell me where Laura is." Shelly buffed her nails against her crisply pressed polo shirt. Examining the tips, she said, "Network wants to interview her." She turned away from Cass, scanning the waterway. "We're looking to interview members of the squad we feel have the best chance to...well, you understand."

"Certainly." Cass swung her gym bag up and over her shoulder. "When I see Laura, tonight, I'll pass along your message. I'm sure she'll be...thrilled."

Shelly caught Cass's arm as she turned away. "Look," she began, "there's no need for us to be adversaries. I have nothing against you, personally."

"Well, isn't that nice. I guess telling your colleagues and the American audience, that I'm 'half-crippled and past my prime' was your way of saying 'let's be friends'?" Cass shook Shelly's hand off her arm. "I don't know how I misunderstood."

"Been listening to my show? How nice."

"I couldn't find the Farm Report."

"You should watch your step with me. And I'd be careful about who you pick for your friends while you're at it." The conciliatory tone was gone, replaced by icy venom.

"Really?" Cass stepped back again and studied the new boathouse and the bustling foot traffic moving in and around the building. She turned again to Shelly, noticing for the first time the small wrinkles peeking through the woman's carefully applied makeup. "I think I'm doing just fine in the friends department, but I'll keep your words in mind, thanks."

"You don't know everything about her, you know."

"Funny, neither do you." Cass cocked her head at Shelly, wondering what her game was. *I don't get it, what is she hoping to accomplish?* Cass decided to push a little. "Okay, so tell me. What is it I don't know?"

A pained look flitted across Shelly's face and immediately her eyes hardened. "She's a bitch and she's responsible for a lot of things. She killed my sister."

The cold voice did little to hide the pain Shelly was obviously still feeling. Cass felt for her—felt for what she must have gone through. When Cass was a kid, still living with her mom in the crappy apartment, their neighbor had killed himself. He'd parked his car in the unit's garage, turned on the engine and had gone to sleep. Cass remembered the guy's family being completely wrecked about the whole thing. She couldn't imagine what it would be like to find your own sister in a pool of blood. There were a lot of "whys" to consider when someone killed themselves, but Cass wasn't willing to let Laura be the scapegoat for anyone.

"Were you hoping I'd be shocked? I thought your sister killed herself." Sadly, Cass shook her head. "I'm sorry for that. For you and for her. But that doesn't make Laura responsible."

"You don't know anything!" Shelly spat out her words, her hands clenched by her sides. "It was *her* fault, she did *nothing* to stop it. And I'll do whatever I can to hurt her the way she hurt me."

Cass turned and strode up the ramp. She still had no idea how she was getting back to the village, or where her team was for that matter, but she wanted to put some distance between herself and Shelly. Quickly. The reporter's chilly tones followed her as she left.

"She's dangerous, you know!"

"Not as dangerous as you are, lady," Cass muttered as she left.

She'd hitchhike back to the village if she needed to, but she wasn't staying around Shelly Michaels any longer.

CHAPTER TWENTY-NINE

"Hey!" Amy frowned as Laura took the steps ahead of her two at a time, she was too short to do the same, and Laura was leaving her in the dust.

"Sorry," Laura laughed breathlessly as she reached the top. She turned and then stepped aside, leaving room for Amy at the top.

Silently cursing her shorter legs, Amy finally topped the last step and then collapsed in a heap at Laura's feet. "I give up. Your kung fu is better than mine," she gasped out between breaths. "I'll never bet you again."

Laura let out a sharp bark of laughter and shook her head. She extended a hand and lifted Amy to her feet. "C'mon short-stuff," Laura slung a friendly arm over Amy's shoulders and steered her around the barricade near the entryway. "Gotta walk it off or you'll stiffen up."

Still trying to catch her breath, Amy just nodded and allowed herself to be led across the flat rooftop. In need of a workout, she'd made the mistake of challenging Laura earlier to some sprints, thinking she'd have an advantage over her, knowing that Laura was more of a distance athlete.

Laura, however, had turned the tables and challenged her to a sprint up the stairs that backed their building. The stairs that ran the *entire height* of the building. What the hell had she been thinking? She glanced over at Laura and frowned when she realized her friend wasn't even winded. Five flights from ground to rooftop. I'm pretty sure she's not human, Amy thought somewhat grumpily as she finished stretching and tipped her head back to down half of the water from the bottle Laura handed her.

It was so breathlessly humid here that she felt it all the way inside. It just sapped her strength. Nearly two months in this climate, first in Japan and now here, and she wondered if she'd ever acclimate. And *she* didn't have to expend the energy that her team did. Looking up again into Laura's flushed features, Amy considered her friend. Long and lean, with a narrow waist and broad shoulders, she looked as if she had adapted just fine to the stifling, sticky heat. Laura, as if sensing Amy's look, turned to face her.

"What?"

Amy shrugged. "Nothin.' "

Laura tilted her head and raised an eyebrow, clearly not convinced.

"Okay, not nothing. I was just wondering how you're doing?"

Laura flashed a grin and leaned back against the wall. She crossed her arms over her chest, pulling the fabric tight across her breasts. Casually lifting her foot, she nudged Amy's leg before crossing her feet at the ankles. "I guess I'm doing pretty good if I can outsprint you." She smiled.

"Ha. Unfair advantage. You didn't tell me we'd be sprinting *up*! Besides, you cheated, you took steps two at a time."

Laura shrugged her broad shoulders. "All's fair in love and war, or something like that." She took another long swallow of her water before turning her head to the east, in the direction of the faraway rowing venue, her lighthearted expression fading slightly.

Amy hopped up onto the wall and absently kicked her heels against the concrete beneath her. She finished her bottle of water and automatically scrunched it up before replacing the cap. She followed Laura's gaze eastward, then poked her friend in the arm. "Hey. Nice try. I want to know, really." She paused and then pushed ahead. "I meant, how are you doing with... everything? Shelly being around has really pissed *me* off, so I was just thinking that—"

"It's fine," Laura said flatly. "I'm fine."

"Laura–"

"Leave it, Ames. I mean it."

Amy shook her head and ignored Laura's forbidding tone. "No. I'm not going to. You're both my friends, you and Cass. And for a while it looked like...well, it looked like she could be good for you. Or you could be good for each other." She took a deep breath and added quietly, "You were...*fun*...again. You were *you* again. And I'd missed you."

Amy held her breath while Laura digested her words, her jaw muscles working as she stared off into the distance. It had seemed too good to be true. She'd watched as Laura first resisted Cass's overtures, rebuffing her to the point of rudeness. But Cass's quiet perseverance had gradually worn away whatever barriers Laura had.

And just when Amy had seen Laura begin to relax, to allow herself to believe...Shelly. That conniving, evil bitch. Amy had never really liked Shelly when she was dating Laura, but since Brenda's death and Shelly's laying all the blame at Laura's feet, Amy's dislike had blossomed into something bordering on hatred. She knew that Laura still carried a great deal of guilt about Brenda's suicide, and this crap with Shelly was bringing it all back.

Laura's jaw tensed again and then she spoke, her words low and bitter. "Seeing her, it's brought it all back. I *know*, I know it wasn't my fault. But...I can't help it. The questions still spin around and around in my head. Did I do enough? Did I miss something? Did I try hard enough to—"

"Laura, you can't keep doing this to yourself."

Laura scrubbed her hands over her face, then turned and rested her elbows on the roughened stone of the low wall. "I hate this."

Amy blinked in surprise. "Hate what?"

"Feeling..." She trailed off and swallowed, her eyes filling.

Amy turned on the wall to face Laura and waited for her to meet her gaze. She could see the pain in Laura's eyes. She was afraid to push, but she knew Laura needed to say it out loud. "Feeling what?" Immediately Laura dropped her gaze and for a long moment she was sure she wasn't going to speak. Amy wondered if she'd pushed too hard. Finally, however, Laura looked up at her again.

"Fragile. I hate feeling fragile. Kind of...broken. I hate that. I hate that she's done that to me. Is doing that to me again."

Pulling in a deep, cleansing breath, Amy turned again toward the boathouse and she felt Laura shift to look the same way. They couldn't see it from here, so she built it in her mind's eye and then began speaking, purposely keeping her voice low and soothing. "Laura, you need to let it go. Let *her*, Brenda, go. All of it." She reached down and laid a hand on her friend's shoulder. "Not just for the team and for tomorrow's race, but for you. You have to find a way." Giving the solidly muscled shoulder beneath her a squeeze, she added, "And just remember, we're all here for you. We've all got your back. Cass too. Especially Cass."

Amy felt more than saw Laura nod in response and realized that was all she'd get right now. And, it was enough. For now.

CHAPTER THIRTY

Amy settled deeper into her seat at the stern and watched as Laura sat, hands easy on the oar as they waited for the start. She tried to clear her mind of everything but the race at hand. Cass had caught her before she left the building and Amy heard Cass's words wash through her as she watched the other boats being eased into position.

"Amy, wait. I just wanted to..." Cass paused, clearly uncertain. She glanced at her watch and then to her erstwhile roommate. "I tried to find Laura earlier and I..." She swallowed and then gave Amy a small smile. "Tear 'em up today, okay?" Before Amy could react, Cass stepped forward and gave her a quick, fierce hug. She whispered, "Pass that on to Laura, would you? And would you tell her that I...that I believe in her? All right?" And then she was gone before Amy could say a word.

Amy hadn't passed on the hug and it was eating at her. She'd been afraid of pulling Laura's focus, just when they needed it to be razor-sharp. Now, however, she was having second thoughts. Amy flicked her gaze to Laura's face to find her staring back, a slightly puzzled expression on her face.

Amy smiled weakly back and then glanced back up the line of boats still easing into position. She had time. She eased forward on the pretext of adjusting her cox-box. "I, um. I forgot to pass something on to you earlier."

One of Laura's eyebrows quirked up as she cocked her head to one side. "What are you talking about?"

"Cass." Amy tugged at her headphones and risked a glance at Laura. She was taking a chance here, but, after seeing the way Laura's face lit up at just the mention of her name, Amy figured she'd made the right choice. "Cass caught me on the way down this morning. Said she'd tried to find you and when she couldn't, she, ah, hugged me."

Now Laura's other eyebrow joined the first. "And this relates to me...how?"

"The hug was for you. She, um, also had a message."

Laura's face grew still and she flexed her fingers once, twice on the oar handle before meeting Amy's gaze and asking softly, "What's the message?"

"She said to tell you that she believes in you."

Amy watched as Laura processed her words, her focus turning inward for a moment as she thought. Then, slowly, a smile slid across her face, relaxing her features and lighting her eyes. When she met Amy's eyes again, her green eyes were bright with a light that Amy hadn't seen for a long time in her friend.

The race referee called for attention and he began polling the boat cox's for readiness. Amy acknowledged his call and then leaned forward. "You good?"

Laura wiped one hand, then the other, on her racing unitard and then settled her hands firmly in place. She gave Amy a quick nod and then glanced over her shoulder. Satisfied that her crew was settled, their oars resting easily on the water and their expressions set, she turned back to Amy, her eyes blazing now in determination. "Yup. Good to go, Ames. Let's do this."

Amy nodded back and waited for the signal. Finally... "Attention!" Then, "Go!"

Amy's entire being was focused on four things; the stroke-rate on her cox-box, the sound of the oars swinging in the locks, the feel of the boat on the water, and the feel of the rhythm of the women before her. Their speed quickly rose in time to her sharp commands to increase the length of their stroke as they neared the first marker. "Three-quarters!" "Full!" "Power ten in two...one! Two!"

With that last command, the team settled into their groove with Amy constantly updating them on their position and that of their competitors. This part of the race never got boring for her, but it was the hardest. Knowing the power drives were yet to come she did her best to conserve the strength of her team. She glanced at Laura's face, the only face she could clearly see among the women. Laura's face told the story. Laura would know what they could and could not do. Laura took her cues from Amy, but Amy also took hers from Laura. Amy shouted "Settle!" and that allowed Laura and the rest of the boat to relax a bit more into their rhythm. She couldn't see all of the other boats, which meant that the U.S. boat was in the lead. They had discussed their strategy earlier, and Amy was sticking to the plan. Win or place second, just enough to qualify without giving away the store.

As they neared the final one-thousand meter mark, Amy heard the German boat's cox shout and glanced over her shoulder to see them inch forward. She caught Laura's eye and nodded, then shouted out another sharp command. Amy didn't fight the tiny thrill that raced through her as the Germans matched their speed; instead she embraced it, used it, and let it fuel the drive in her as she continued to shout encouragement to her team.

"Ready, power ten in two! One...two!" Amy called the signal for the last ten strokes and knew they had it in the bag. They'd made the medal rounds. As they crossed the line the referee's horn blast signaled their finish and Amy directed them to "Let 'er run!" allowing the long boat to bleed off speed after the finish. She high-fived Laura and then watched as Laura, like the rest of the women in her crew, lay back against the legs of the woman behind her. They sucked in air and listened as the referee's horn continued to signal other boats crossing the line. Those who didn't finish in the top two were out, this time for good.

Finally Laura sat up and reached forward to pull Amy into a hug as best she could in the narrow confines of their craft. "Great job, Ames. Great job!"

"You too! We're in the A Final, Laura! We're going to the medal round!" Amy's glee was infectious, and as the women recovered from their efforts, the jubilation spread and they began laughing and high-fiving each other. Amy efficiently guided the boat back to the docks, keeping the crew in check as much as she could.

Amy glanced from the docks to the crowded stands. She could just make out the rest of the U.S. squad gathered at the end of the run, in the athletes area before the stands. From this distance she couldn't really make out individuals. She did, however, wave to them as the boat glided smoothly past.

"Port side, watch your blades," she called. As the boat eased into the dock, Amy ordered, "Port oars to the gunnels and lean away," and Laura and the other three women on the port side pulled their oars in until the blades rested against the rigging. Amy automatically checked to be sure they turned the blade flat as they leaned, allowing the blade and rigging to clear the low dock. The rest of the process of extricating herself from the boat was done by rote as the crew deftly followed her commands. Finally, she was able to free herself from the tiny confines of her cox space and stretch.

"Here," a soft voice said, catching her attention. Amy looked up to see Cass's sparkling brown eyes above her. She watched as Laura handed off her oar and stepped dockside, careful to do so in sync with her crew, lest they end their terrific finish with an ignominious wet-down by tipping the long boat. Cass steadied Laura as the dock shifted with the new weight, and Laura slipped her hand over Cass's, the small action bringing a smile to Amy's face. Once everyone was out and the support staff took charge of the boat, she let herself enjoy the moment.

In an uncharacteristic show of enthusiasm, Laura spun and swept Cass up in a hug, spinning them both around. She then set her aside and advanced on Amy, a wide grin on her face.

"C'mon, Ames! You know the drill!"

Amy yelped and dove behind Cass. "No! Laura! You can't toss me yet, that's for the finals!"

The rest of the crew gathered around and looked to Laura who grinned again and then cocked her head toward Cass. "What do you think? Toss her, or not?"

Cass laughed as Amy clutched at the back of her shirt. She reached back to pat her roommate on the arm reassuringly. "I'm pretty sure you need to save that for the big finish, Laura."

"Thanks, Cass," Amy whispered, still not releasing her hold on Cass's polo shirt, just in case.

Amidst mock groans of disappointment from her team, Laura nodded. She reached again for Amy and pulled her from behind Cass, then slung her arm over both women's shoulders. "Fair enough. But," she warned, with a mock glare at Amy, "get ready, Ames, 'cause in two days you're going flyin.' "

Amy enjoyed the laughter and banter of her team as they celebrated their finish to the finals, and she was thrilled when she looked over to find Laura smiling warmly down at Cass. She was suddenly very glad she'd passed on Cass's message at the last minute, sure that had done the job.

CHAPTER THIRTY-ONE

Cass and Yanmei gently set the long, sleek boat on the padded wooden cradle, carefully holding it until it was balanced properly. She quietly thanked the sweet security guard, making a mental note to sign a team cap for her later in the week. Cass had talked Coach into letting her take the van out after dinner, needing to have some quiet time before tomorrow's doubles finals. The medals races for the eights had been pushed back two days, meaning that Cass and Sarah were finally racing in the morning, after a two-day delay.

Cass couldn't really believe it. They'd blown through the semifinal heats almost too easily and it all seemed...surreal. She mentally reviewed the teams she and Sarah would face. They would be up against the best tomorrow, and she wanted to give their scull one last once-over before the morning's races.

Gently sliding the bow seat up and back along the slide, Cass closed her eyes and felt for any unevenness in the movement. She added a bit more light grease to the left runner and ran the seat again. This time there was no hesitation in the seat's progress. She did the same for the stern seat, adding grease where it was needed.

She worked in the near-darkness, tweaking the shell, making minute adjustments, lit only by the lone bulb glowing high above the racks of stacked and prepped boats. The single light cast harsh shadows, and she had to lean sideways to see what she was doing. The boathouse was nearly empty, just one or two other athletes or team assistants quietly prepping their equipment before tomorrow's races.

Cass worked methodically, letting her mind wander. She could feel her nerves rising and to combat them began to build the day ahead in her mind. Piece by piece she added elements, beginning first with the water. It always started there. Then came the boathouse. The undulating shape of the roof, the gentle sweep of the natural bank leading to the water, the perfect man-made straightaway that was the venue for their final qualifying heat in the morning.

Tomorrow is it. That thought winged its way through her thoughts. Shaking her head, she closed her eyes and added details to her visualization. The lap of water against the sides of the shell, the slap of oars hitting the water in near-perfect synchronization, the thunk and slide, point-counter-point of the seats and the oarlocks accompanying the rhythm of the boat's movement through the water. She even added the tangy, salty air, the flavor of it scratchy against the back of her throat as she sucked in air. She saw the vee they cut through the water, pointing them on toward victory.

Cass's vision was so complete, so detailed, that she lost herself in the moment. She was no longer in the darkened boathouse, but instead living in the space she'd created in her mind. Her boat, she and Sarah charging down the lane to the finish. She let herself imagine the relief and the joy she'd feel as they swept to victory. And a tiny part of her added one last element to the fantasy. She imagined the joy and pride on Laura's face as she, along with the rest of the U.S. squad, watched Cass's boat triumph. So intently was she focused on her own preparations that she lost track of time and those around her. She was startled by a voice coming from someone immediately behind her in the dark.

"Back again? Why do I always find you here alone?"

"Excuse me?" Cass peered into the darkness, trying to locate the speaker. She shaded her eyes from the overhead light and moved away from her boat. "Oh, for cryin' out...Shelly? What do you *want*?"

"Just came to give you a message." The shadows shifted and Shelly stepped out. She casually pulled a towel from the side of the shell and wiped her hands. "Stay away from Laura."

Cass grabbed a towel of her own, wiping the excess grease off her hands. She stepped around the boat, putting some distance between herself and Shelly. *Shit, the woman's nuts.* She took another step, trying to figure out how she could attract Yanmei's attention, or anybody's for that matter. She watched as Shelly stepped closer and stopped, resting her hands on the dark blue hull of her boat.

"Get your hands off my boat."

"What?" Shelly looked down, then shrugged as if to say the shell was of no importance to her. "Fine. Whatever. Did you hear what I said?"

"Yes, I heard you. I don't know what you're talking about."

"I said, stay away from Laura."

"Yeah, I got that. I don't see how that's any of your business."

"It is my business. *Laura* is my business. If you're smart, you'll stay clear of her."

"I don't believe this." Cass shook her head, tucking her hair behind her ears. "Are you *threatening* me? You have got to be kidding."

"It's no threat, it's a promise. If you know what's good for you, you'll stay away from her."

"Right, then. That's it. Yanmei!" Cass called out suddenly, startling Shelly into stepping back. She nodded to the small security guard who raced around the corner and slid to a stop before her.

"Yes, Miss?" Yanmei's breathless voice was high, and she glanced nervously between Cass and Shelly.

"Yanmei, this woman should not be in here, she is not a member of any team."

"Oh! But she say—"

"Oh, be quiet," Shelly snapped. She waved her press credential and gestured to the now flustered security guard. "I have every right to be here."

The security guard grabbed it and examined it carefully. She flushed bright red before giving it back.

"No, Miss. Your pass not for inside. Please, come?"

Yanmei placed her hand on Shelly's arm and attempted to lead her toward the door. Shelly yanked herself free and raised a hand to strike the young guard. Suddenly, her hand was caught in a vise-like grip.

"I don't think so." Cass's voice was low, angry.

Shelly struggled for a moment before swearing and relaxing her arm. Cass nodded and slowly released the woman's hand, keeping her body between Shelly's and Yanmei's. "I guess I'm in better shape than you expected, hmm?"

Shelly yanked her shirt straight and spun around, heading for the exit. "This isn't over, bitch. I warned you."

Oh my God, the woman really is nuts.

Cass waited until Shelly was out the door before turning to Yanmei. She was trembling now from the adrenaline and she could see the little security guard was in the same shape.

"Yanmei, are you okay?"

"Yes, Miss. I so sorry. She has badge, and I see her with you and others, so I think..." She wrung her hands together in distress. "Please, I am sorry. I will be sure she does not return in here."

"Thank you, Yanmei."

"Yes," another voice said out of the darkness. "Thank you, Yanmei for your help."

Laura stepped from the shadows, concern on her face. She watched Yanmei return to her post, then turned to Cass.

"Are *you* okay?"

Flustered, Cass simply nodded. She'd spent a laughter-filled evening with Laura after the eight's win three days ago, but since then had barely seen her. Laura could—and did—disappear for hours at a time, a habit that in turns frustrated and intrigued Cass. She looked up to find Laura staring at her intently. "How much did you hear?"

"Enough that I'm worried. What was she doing in here?"

"I don't know. She came out of the dark and basically told me to stay away from you."

"Cass, you know she's not my girlfriend, right?"

"Oh God, I hope not. You'd have to have your head examined to be with—" Cass stopped, realizing what she was saying. "Damn, Laura, I didn't mean that."

"Yes you did, but it's okay. She wasn't always—" Laura stopped and shook her head. She looked over the boat and then up at Cass. "About finished here?"

At Cass's nod, the two women lifted the shell back into its storage cradle. They gathered up the wax, grease and oil and tucked it into the storage box at the end of their team's section. Together they walked out to where Cass had parked the van. Cass started to get in, but stopped when Laura put a hand on her arm.

"Cass, look. Maybe it would be better if we..." Laura stopped, her eyes shadowed by the night, her voice reflecting her struggle. "We've gotten to be friends and I, um, *like* that. Like you. But maybe it's better if we...if you stay away from me for a while."

The humid night air seemed suddenly thicker to Cass. She struggled to get a deep breath...Laura's words had knocked the wind out of her. *I...she...no. She's going to let that woman mess up this thing we have. That we might have.*

"Laura," she said softly. "No."

"Yes, Cass. I mean it."

"I don't get you, you know? You run hot, then cold. One minute you're hugging me like...like it means something—"

"It—"

"No, let me. Then...you just disappear. I don't know whether I'm coming or going. Or whether *you're* coming or going."

Laura ran her hands through her hair, tangling the red waves into disarray. She opened her mouth and then snapped it shut again. She waved a hand between them, "See? This is what I mean. This is why I..."

"What, because I'm frustrated with you? No. You want to back off because your ex is here and she's stirring things up." Cass took a deep breath and stepped forward. "Look, I like you. I think we make a pretty good team. Whatever else, we're *friends*, Laura. You can't let her do this to you, to our friendship." Cass took both of Laura's hands in hers, noting how cold her fingers were. "You can't. I won't let you."

Laura pulled her hands free and stepped back. Cass could see that she was trembling, and ached for her.

"It's not your decision. There's something broken with her, and I won't let that touch you."

She stepped out of the ring of the streetlight, leaving Cass alone near the van. Her softly spoken, "I'm sorry," drifted back on the damp night breeze, bringing Cass little comfort.

CHAPTER THIRTY-TWO

Amy glanced again at the door to the room she'd shared with Cass. Cass had retreated there to dress earlier, and Amy had given her time alone to prepare for the day's race. Today's event was the final medal round for the double sculls and Amy knew Cass was nervous as a cat this morning. She'd watched as Cass tried to settle herself with some stretching exercises before giving up and going to change. Amy had hoped that Laura would be able to settle her friend down. It seemed as if the two had grown closer, especially following the Eight's spectacular finish in the repechage. The two had been inseparable at dinner that night. But Amy frowned as she realized that she hadn't seen the two together since then. Now that she thought about it, she hadn't seen Laura with Cass for several days. *Damn.* She grabbed her sneakers and knocked on the dorm door.

"Hey, can I come in?"

"Sure. I'm almost ready."

Amy bounced over to Cass, reaching to grab her gym bag as they left their room.

"How do you feel?"

"Good. Fine. Okay."

Amy chuckled, then said, "Um, wanna pick one?"

Cass's wan smile stretched a bit further. "Sure. I'll go with okay."

"Hmm, have to do something about that."

She watched Cass's surreptitious check of the main room, knowing that she was looking for Laura. They were the only ones left in the common room, the rest of the squad having gone ahead to the venue. Amy led Cass to the elevators.

"She left a little while ago."

"Who?"

"Come on, Cass. I know you're looking for Laura. What happened?"

"Nothing."

Outside, Sheila waved them over to the team van, checking her watch one more time.

"All set?"

"Yeah."

"Good. Sarah's with Pam and Josh," she said, referring to Cass's double scull partner and two of the assistant coaches. "They're getting the numbers from the referee. There's been some last-minute rearranging or something. Computer glitch."

Sheila's speech was as choppy and short as Cass's, and Amy knew it had to do with today's medal round. She knew that when the Eight went later in the week she'd be just as nervous and short. Amy said nothing for a moment as the coach began the drive to the boathouse, then tried again with Cass.

"You know, she's just as miserable as you are."

"She's got a funny way of showing it. Shit, Amy, she cut me off. I thought we had something...something good. She let that... that bitch decide for us." Cass shrugged, resigned. "I resent it and I'm hurt."

The two watched the scenery slide by in silence. Finally, Cass turned to Amy.

"You know what, Amy? That's what really gets me. *She* decided for *us*. Laura simply decided that since Shelly threatened to make things tough for me, it would be best to stay away from each other. No discussion, no alternatives. It makes me wonder if that's the real reason, you know?"

"What do you mean?"

"What if...what if Shelly's just an excuse? God Ames, I was really falling for her. What if she just didn't feel the same way? God, I'm *such* an idiot sometimes."

Amy reached out and caught Cass's hand in her own. This wasn't the time for any of this and she didn't know any other way to offer comfort. She simply sat there and held her friend's hand, wishing for the right words.

Sheila pulled the van into the reserved slots and waited for Amy to get out. She caught Cass's arm before they left the van.

"Cass. Put it aside for now and focus. I need you to do that. Sarah needs it too. Okay?"

Cass nodded reluctantly, and they joined Amy on the sidewalk. As the trio made their way down to the launching area, a red-jacketed official approached Sheila, accompanied by Josh, one of the team's assistant coaches.

"Uh-oh." Amy pulled Cass to a halt.

"What?" Cass's voice was tight with tension.

"I don't like the look of this."

Amy and Cass watched the official confer with the coach. After a minute, the official left and Sheila turned to Cass. She ran a hand through her close-cropped hair and frowned.

"Ames, run down and get Sarah, okay? Meet us at the course referee's office."

Amy nodded and ran off. Whatever was going on was not good.

Sheila waved Cass and Josh forward. All three followed the race official to the tower.

CHAPTER THIRTY-THREE

"You think I *what?*" Cass stood, rigid with indignation, as she faced the chief referee. The room had gone silent after his announcement, and she was certain that everyone in the room could hear her heart banging in her chest.

"As I say, there is no evidence, simply an allegation." The official bowed to her, but his voice was disapproving.

"But I—"

"An allegation made by whom?" Sheila's voice drowned out Cass's protests. She placed a hand on Cass's shoulder, squeezing to silence her. The official looked from Sheila to Cass and back again. He looked extremely uncomfortable and distressed. As he opened his mouth to speak, the door swung open and Amy, Sarah and someone Cass didn't know entered the room. Sheila, however, recognized the man instantly.

"Kevin, thank God. Cass? This is Kevin Taylor, of the U.S.O.C. Kev, this is Cass Flynn. Can you help us sort this out?"

"I hope so, Sheila." The slender representative of the United States Olympic Committee looked upset and angry. Tall and slim, with hair that at one time had been red and was now a faded gingery-orange, he was the image of a metrosexual. He had the look of an athlete, though, and that reassured Cass, as did his confident tone when he turned to the official and began a rapid exchange in Chinese. Cass stood next to Sarah, both women holding hands and anxiously watching the exchange.

"What's going on?" Sarah whispered.

"I'm not sure. The ref says *somebody*," and she made air quotes with her free hand to emphasize her point, "says I was seen tampering with the Irish boat."

"But that's crazy!"

"Yeah, I know. And I'll bet I know where the...allegation... comes from."

"Who—"

Sheila cleared her throat as Taylor turned toward them, his face grim. He pulled out a chair and waved everyone to sit as the Chinese official opened the door and spoke rapidly to someone in the outer office. Everyone but Sheila sat. The coach remained where she was, legs planted shoulder-width apart, arms crossed. She exuded anger, and her presence, so firmly behind them, bolstered Cass. The official joined them at the table, passing a pitcher of water around. Cass glanced at the clock on the wall. Two hours before the start of the race.

She started to ask a question, then stopped as Taylor shook his head. His eyes were sharp behind the steel-framed lenses that rested on his pointed nose. "Ms. Flynn, if you'll wait until the others get here?"

Cass nodded, her eyes on her hands clasped tightly together on the table in front of her. She knew who had done this, she was certain of it. *I should have reported her threat last night. Damn. Now if I say something they'll think I'm making it up.*

Beside her, Amy nudged her shoulder, offering silent comfort. Sarah sat to her right, still and silent, almost vibrating with anger. She could feel the solid presence of Sheila standing behind her. It seemed like hours before the door opened again, this time to admit the Irish coach and doubles team. All three looked perplexed and the two rowers somewhat anxious.

The taller of the two Irish rowers relaxed when she spotted Sarah.

"Sarah, what the devil is going on?"

"Alanna. I don't know, really. This is Cass. Cass, Alanna Doyle, bow seat—"

"Ladies, have a seat." Taylor cleared his throat as the rowers sat. The coach, however, stood behind her team, mirroring Sheila's pose. "Coach McCandless, the chief referee says that allegations have been made, accusing a member of the U.S. women's doubles team of tampering with your boat's rigging."

Taylor acknowledged the Irish team's gasps of surprise with a nod. Coach McCandless's eyes flickered between Cass and Sarah, then up to Sheila. Her face flushed with anger and her jaw tightened. Before she could speak, Taylor raised his hand.

"I take it you know nothing of these charges?"

McCandless shook her head, restraining Doyle in her seat. The rower was visibly upset, her eyes too flicking from Sarah to Cass and back again.

"I've heard nothing of this, have you Alanna? Kay?"

"Nothing!" Alanna shook off her coach's hand and jumped to her feet. She began to pace the length of the room. "This is rubbish! Sarah wouldn't—they would do nothing of the sort!"

McCandless nodded and addressed the chief referee. "I will, of course, check our rigging carefully. But, well, to be honest, I simply do not believe that what you have heard is true." The Irish coach looked around the room. "Where is your witness?"

The official bowed to McCandless. "I have no name to offer you, Coach. It was only a message that was passed on to my office."

"You dragged four women who have to compete in less than two hours into your office to talk about something that you're not even certain took *place*?" Disgusted disbelief colored

McCandless's words. She turned to Sheila and simply shook her head.

Sheila nodded to the Irish coach, a small smile on her face. "Thank you, Siobhan, for your faith in us." She dusted her hands on her sweats and turned to the referee and said curtly, "We're done here." Cass could hear the suppressed fury in her voice as she waved Cass and Sarah to their feet. "Now. Since there seems to be no wronged party here, perhaps you can tell me what started this? While," she held up a hand, "my athletes, along with these women, continue their preparation for the upcoming race?"

The chief referee glanced around the room, hesitating for a moment before finally nodding in agreement. Cass and the others quickly left, leaving Sheila and Taylor in the room with the Chinese official. In the hallway, Alanna gave Sarah a quick hug. The two obviously knew each other well.

"Jaysus, Mary and Joseph, Sarah, what in the hell was all that about, do you think?"

Sarah shook her head and glanced quickly at Cass. At her nod, Sarah said, "We think someone's out to smear Cass. Throw her off her game."

"You'd be speaking of the woman who's been so spiteful on the radio then?"

"Yes, we think so."

"Is this related to the troubles your eight had the other day?"

Cass looked at Amy and then nodded, wondering if Coach had put the two incidents together yet.

"That *bitch*." Amy spit out. "She was all over last night's broadcast, too, making nasty comments about teams cheating!"

"Well, God help you if she's got the media in her corner!" Alanna turned to Cass. "Sorry, our introduction was cut a bit short. We've met before, haven't we?"

"Oh, sorry. Cass, Alanna Doyle and Kay Sinclair. Alanna, Cass Flynn." Sarah nudged Amy's shoulder and shook her head, trying to calm her down.

Cass answered Alanna. "Yes, we met after Nationals, but there were a lot of people there."

"Yes, I remember, you're from one of the states in the middle, aren't you?"

"Wisconsin. Yes. Glad to meet you, ah, again." Cass blew out a breath. The brief interlude with the Irish scullers served to distract Cass for a moment, allowing her to get some of her anger under control. She looked up at the Irish coach. "Sorry about the mess, Coach."

"Not your fault then, is it?" McCandless waved off Cass's apology as she led them back down to the launching area. The Irish coach waved her athletes toward their boat, then turned to Sarah and Cass.

"Sarah, Alanna's spoken of you, well and often. I am happy that we could help you out today and very sorry for your troubles. Good luck to you both."

"And to you," Sarah said. "Thanks again for your support, we really appreciate it."

Both women watched as McCandless made her way to the emerald green shell and her team. Sarah tucked her arm in Cass's and steered them toward their own boat. "You know, of course, that it was that bitch Michaels behind this, don't you?"

"Yeah."

"Well, I guess one thing she hadn't counted on were our close ties to the team she accused you of tampering with!"

"What do you mean?"

Sarah laughed and said, "Well, Alanna is my ex-girlfriend and," she paused, looking back over her shoulder at the Irish coach, "rumor has it Coach Sheila and McCandless were quite the hot item back in the day."

Cass's laughter blended with Sarah's, her nerves and tension suddenly gone. Shelly Michaels' spiteful and rather pitiful attempt to derail her had failed. Even better, it had served to push Cass's focus from herself to her boat where it should have been in the first place. Her nerves were gone, now. In their place was pure, fiery determination. She grabbed her gym bag and sat on the docks to pull off her sandals, using the ritual to refocus on the upcoming race. She methodically placed her sandals into the bag and as she slipped her hand in deeper in search of her crew socks, her fingers brushed a small piece of paper. Curious, she pulled it out and unfolded it.

Cass,

I know it seems pretty high school to be leaving you a note, but I couldn't find you when I got down to the docks. Anyway. I just wanted to let you know that I'm thinking of you and I know you'll go all the way today. I'd like to talk when you're done today. When you've WON! You're a hell of an addition to the team and I'm glad you're here. For a lot of reasons.

Remember, "Who do you play for?!"

Thinking of you,

LK

A slow smile spread across Cass's face, matching the warmth blossoming inside. She'd remembered. Laura had remembered a conversation they'd had weeks ago, just after their elevator do-over. They'd argued about the all-time best sports movie ever, finally agreeing that the story of the men's hockey team's 1980 "Miracle" win capped them all. Herb Brooks' inspiring question to his team, "Who do you play for?" and their shouted "USA!" response had become Laura and Cass's private training mantra. When Cass would falter, Laura would ask it and Cass would do the same in return. Over the weeks, the rest of the team had picked it up as well, using it as a rallying cry that worked to fire them all up.

Cass read through the note again, running her fingers over the last words in the note, savoring the words on the page one more time before tucking the paper safely back into her gym bag. She'd come to terms, somewhat, with her attraction. Or so she thought. She'd decided to wait Laura out, sure that eventually she would come to her. With the medal races to focus on she hadn't wanted to distract either of them, so she'd just...let it be. And now...now it looked like that approach was paying off. Suddenly Cass felt buoyant, invincible.

Screw Shelly Michaels and her petty gamesmanship. *You can't touch me, bitch. And after I win this, we'll just see what else I go after.*

CHAPTER THIRTY-FOUR

The wake they cut through the water was the only thing Cass saw. Not the other shells, not the swiftly receding start line, not the chase boats. Nothing but the tips of her foot stop and the V they were cutting through the water. Behind her she could hear Sarah's sharp huff! each time she caught the water with her oars. Cass's breathing hitched when Sarah's did.

Exactly when Sarah's did.

Perfectly in sync.

They had it.

The swing. That often-elusive cadence that epitomizes the absolute synchronization between rowers. She could feel the electricity in the air. Hear the growing roar of the crowd still muffled under the rhythmic sweep of hers and Sarah's oars as they swept toward the finish.

Inch by inch they moved forward, distancing themselves from those they were leaving, quite literally, in their wake. Trailing them were the Brits, the French and the Italians. Before their shell lay the finish line and two crews, the Dutch and the Irish. Cass knew that when she could see the stands to her left they'd have only one thousand meters to the finish. Time and distance were running out.

Catch the water with the oar, *pull through* in the drive using the legs, with the arms straight out until almost at full extension, then pull the arms back into the chest, *lay back* to finish the stroke, *release* the oars from the water, feather or twist the oar so it's more aerodynamic and *recover*, sliding forward into the tucked crouch to begin again. *Catch, pull through, lay back, release, feather aaaaand recover. Catch, pull through, lay back, release, feather aaaaand recover.* Cutting through the noise of the shell slicing through the water, the hard thunk of the oarlock and the swelling noise of the spectators, was Coach's voice, drilling that cadence into her head.

Every muscle in Cass's body screamed for oxygen, her legs felt like dead weights, her arms leaden. *Catch, pull through, lay back, release, feather aaaaand recover.* She could see the three boats pushing toward her, which meant there were still two between their shell and the finish, two between her and a gold medal. She let out a shout, "Sarah?"

"We go in two!"

"Counting...one..." *Catch, pull through, lay back, release, feather aaaaand recover.* "...and two!" With that shout, Cass and Sarah dug in and turned it on.

Nine hundred ninety meters ahead, the U.S. squad led the crowd's roar as the tiny blue shell seemed to shoot forward suddenly. Sheila watched as Laura stood, her body unconsciously swaying to the rhythm created by the two in the shell, and muttered to herself as the shell surged forward.

"Too soon, Sarah, too soon!" Laura muttered, louder this time. She shifted forward on the bench, hardly aware of her white-knuckled grip on the rail in front of her. Sheila glanced at the screen and, like Laura, was sure that Sarah had called the final push too soon. There was no way she and Cass could hold that stroke rate to the finish. They had not even reached the stands yet and that meant they'd have to hold their finish rate of forty strokes per minute for just under one thousand meters.

It was impossible.

Nobody does that. Hell, the men row at thirty-six until the last five hundred and that's in a *fast* race!

Sheila glanced again at the finish, then at the shells seeming to creep toward it. *It always goes much faster when I'm on the water, not watching.* Frustrated with the distance and the impossibility of seeing who was moving up, Sheila glanced again at the giant JumboTron screen dominating the inland side of the run. Squinting against the bright sun, she pulled her team cap lower to block the glare and tried desperately to see where Cass's boat was now. *They're gaining.* Gauging the distance again, Sheila resisted the urge to kick the rail before her. *Maybe...* Suddenly the gap between the tiny blue shell and the lead boat seemed too great to overcome and the distance to the finish too little to make their run. *They're out of room, their start pace was too slow. Oh damn, poor Cass. C'mon...* She looked again at Laura and saw the tension in her face. *Poor Laura, too.*

If it were possible to pull the tiny boat forward with the force of her stare, the U.S. shell would have no problem gaining victory. Laura's eyes stayed locked on the blue arrow slicing through the mild, rippling current, on the smaller figure at the back of the shell. Sheila could see their rhythm, their sync. The athlete in her marveled at the skill the two were displaying. To mesh so well and so quickly, it was amazing. This race had been almost a throwaway after Pam's injury, but now, with Cass and the renewed energy of the team, it looked as if they had a chance. Or *had* one.

Like a wave pushed before the wind, the roar of the crowd grew louder as the tiny shells moved into the viewing stand area. Where seconds before the boats seemed to be crawling along, now they seemed to be going impossibly fast. Sheila couldn't see their faces but knew at this moment what all the women were thinking. Or rather, what they weren't thinking. This was the moment athletes trained for, worked for and dreamed of. This was *it*, that mythical "two strikes, bottom of the ninth, bases loaded" moment Olympians imagined as children when taking their first, tentative steps on the path to the Games. Right now, Cass and Sarah were focused on just one thing: getting every second of speed from their boat, every ounce of strength from their bodies and making up that seemingly impossible distance to finish in the money.

Sheila was jostled as the other team members crowded around her, yelling their support to the women on the water. She pressed a hand down onto Laura's shoulder, the fingers of her other hand white from the pressure of her grip on the rail.

"Can they make it?" Laura's voice was low, tense.

"I don't... I can't see... Oh my GOD!" Sheila's shout snapped Laura's gaze from the JumboTron screen back to the boats racing toward them.

Impossibly, the ball mounted on the front of the blue U.S. boat in Lane 3 was inching past the Dutch boat. Bit by bit, the bright yellow bow ball moved past the bow of the Dutch scull, Cass and Sarah in perfect sync, driving their shell forward. Just inches ahead of them and two lanes to their left, was the Irish boat, its bright green hull flashing in the sun.

On the water, Sarah heard the Irish sternman step up their rate, signaling the approach of the last five hundred meters of the race.

"Cass! Let's roll!"

Cass's only response was to lower her head and dig in. They'd rehearsed this sprint to the finish several times in the last month, but never at this rate. *Time to go.*

I can do this. We can do this. Clenching her teeth, Cass matched Sarah's slightly longer arc, making the stroke that tiny bit longer, carrying the boat that little bit further. Rowing faster was not always about adding another stroke or two per minute, it was also about technique. The longer the stroke, the farther the boat traveled.

Row smarter, not harder.

Okay, do both.

Cass lengthened her backswing and deepened her position at the catch for a deeper drive in time with her teammate. Sarah let out a shout as their boat surged ahead, responding to their extra effort.

Three hundred fifty meters to the finish.

The crowd surged to its feet, stomping and yelling at the finish. Today's event was proving more exciting than anyone had expected. Beside the U.S. squad on the rail, the Dutch team members were screaming and waving their flag, trying to bring their women back into the race.

Sheila scowled at them and yelled louder. She knew Sarah and Cass couldn't hear her over the distance, or above the sound of their oars hitting the rigging, or even over the sound of their breathing at this point. Nevertheless, she added her voice to the cacophony of noise surrounding the finish. A sharp elbow in her side forced her to step aside.

"Dammit coach, I can't *see*!" Amy shoved and elbowed her way to the front, the tiny cox nearly jumping out of her sneakers in her attempts to see over her taller teammates. Laura grabbed her by the shoulders and wedged Amy into a small space between herself and Sheila, right on the rail. On the water, the sleek blue scull gained another foot on the Irish boat, Sarah's bow seat now even with Ireland's stern rower. Amy's wince was visible as Laura tightened her grip on her shoulder. It was like watching a tennis match; first the Irish boat had the lead, then the Americans, then the Irish. Amy clenched her fists and pounded them on the rail. "*C'mon ladies*! Haul ass!"

Two hundred meters to the finish.

Cass was certain this was the longest race she'd ever been in.

We've been rowing for days. Dig in Cass, dig in.

The thump and bang of the oars against the oarlocks began a counterpoint rhythm to the sound of the water rushing against the hull as they moved forward. Cass gained a seat-length on the Irish hull. She began singing in her head. Rounds of that endless children's tune began to work their way through her tired cells. *Row, row, row your boat, gently down the stream...*

One hundred meters to go.

Cass drew even with the forward rower in the Irish boat. *We're there! Sarah's gotta be even with their bow ball, we're in front.* She heard a shout as the stroke for the Irish boat pushed their rate higher. The Irish boat shot forward again. Cass shook her head.

No way.

No. Fucking. Way.

"Ten in two, Cass! Ready? One...Two!"

Cass nodded and dug in as Sarah did. This was the call she'd been waiting for. The call for the last ten strokes in the race. As hard as they'd been pulling since the one thousand-meter mark, *now* they poured it on. This was where mental conditioning made all the difference, where races were won or lost. Now, when your body was tired beyond imagining and you felt as if you'd rowed for weeks. It was not the strength of the body that finished the race. It was the strength of the mind, the mental ability to dredge up that last reserve of energy.

Eyes slitted against the sweat pouring down past her cap, Cass shut it all out. The damp, fishy smell of the air; the growing cheers of the crowd; the thunk of the oars in the oarlocks; the hiss of the slides and the voices of the scullers in the nearby Irish shell.

Ten.

From deep inside, Cass called on those reserves.

Nine.

There it was, that euphoria. That zing. *I could fly if I wanted to.*

Eight.

Cass was suddenly aware of the tiniest details. She could

hear Sarah's breathing behind her, louder than any other sound around her.

Seven.

One of the laces holding her right foot in the foot stop had come free and seemed to float in its own gravity as she slid forward for the next catch.

Six.

The orange lane markers flashed past in a strobe-like blur.

Five.

A flash to her right of sunlight catching the water on her oar's blade.

Four.

A glance up, back along the lane, a snapshot burned in her memory.

Three.

Sarah's grunt as her oars caught the water. A glimpse of Irish green to her left.

Two.

The whistle of the wind they were making. An odd shooshing sound she only ever heard on the water. Another flash of emerald green. A shout from the stands.

One.

Catch, pull through, lay back, release, feather aaaaand...

"Let 'er run, Cass! Let 'er run!" Sarah's call to stop rowing heralded both women's collapse backward in the shell, struggling for breath. The blast of the finish horn drowned out her words. It was followed almost instantaneously by another burst, as first one boat then another crossed the finish line. A third blast, as the bronze medalists crossed the line, only vaguely registered with Cass as she fought for air. The double-blast of the first two finishers told Cass that it was too close to know who'd won, they'd have to wait for the official call.

CHAPTER THIRTY-FIVE

The loud blasts of the horns signaling the end of the race startled Sheila even though she was expecting them. It was impossible to tell who'd finished first and she, like everyone in the crowd, turned to the giant screen to view the finish again as it was replayed. Everyone was speculating on the final result.

"They did it."

"Damn, looks like the Irish got 'em in the end."

"Hell of a finish, eh? Who'd have thought that..."

"Wow. Look at *that*!"

Sheila tuned them all out, concentrating all of her attention on the large screen. It sure as hell looked to her as if they'd done it. God they *deserved* it, they'd worked so damned hard for it. She'd never seen a team row that fast for that long. She wondered if they'd set some sort of course record today, she was pretty sure she'd never seen a double scull race that fast in her life.

Out on the water, with nothing propelling it forward, their little blue shell drifted to a relative standstill in the water, along with the other two top finishers. Cass turned and reached backward for Sarah, the two women laughing and crying together.

"Oh my God, what a race!"

"That was *awesome*!"

"How'd we finish? Could you tell?"

Sarah shrugged. "Dunno. I think...I'm not sure, really." Turning slightly, she shouted to the women collapsed in the emerald shell next to them. "Alanna! Great race! Too bad about the gold!"

Untangling herself from her partner, Alanna Doyle laughed and shouted back, "In yer dreams Yank!" She tipped her head to Cass. "Well done to you."

Cass grinned back at the woman Sarah had introduced as an ex-girlfriend. "Thanks." She bent to loosen the laces on her shoes and was distracted by a roar from the crowd. Suddenly Sarah was pounding her back and shouting, "We did it! We did it!" Pulled backward into Sarah's enthusiastic embrace, Cass turned to the JumboTron to see the photo finish of the race.

Sarah was right.

They had done it.

By a ball.

Cass squinted to make the suddenly shimmering screen come into clearer focus. She could hear the tinny voice of the announcer carrying over the water, making the results official.

"*...the results, in order of finish, are: United States, gold; Republic of Ireland, silver; and the Netherlands, bronze.*"

The announcer's voice was drowned out by the shouts from the stands and the other boats on the water. Cass turned back to the loading area below the stands, scanning for her teammates. Sarah pulled her around a bit more and pointed. "There they are, over there." Her arm extended behind her, Sarah pointed to the crowd of laughing, shouting women excitedly waving them in.

Cass laughed, spotting Amy jumping up and down wildly as she hugged everyone in her vicinity. Next to Amy stood Coach Sheila and Laura, both women grinning and laughing at Amy's antics. As Cass watched, Laura turned toward the water and lifted a hand. Cass waved and turned back in her seat, fishing for her oar handles, ready to head in to collect some well-deserved hugs.

CHAPTER THIRTY-SIX

Sheila dropped her hand back to the railing, grinning as her team celebrated the unexpected and hard-won victory. Around her people were shouting and laughing, letting the adrenaline of the exciting finish run its course. A shout went up and the announcer confirmed her private musings.

"Ladies and gentlemen, we also have a new Olympic and course record of..."

Whatever else he had to say was lost in a sea of jubilant shouts as the U.S. squad increased their cheers. If possible, Amy began leaping higher than she had during the race, running through their team and those nearby, demanding high-fives. Sheila crossed her arms and grinned, delighted with her team's performance and thrilled with the victory. Laura nudged her shoulder and tilted her head out toward the water.

"Whaddya say, Coach?"

Sheila just shook her head, her smile getting wider. "What do I think? I think this is one hell of a regatta, don't you?"

Laura laughed and nodded, as she slapped the coach on the back. "You know what? I think you're right!" She looked across the water again and spotted the two women in the blue scull looking her way. Raising a hand to wave again, she gasped and grabbed Sheila's arm. "Shit, crab, CRAB!" Laura's frantic voice cut through the jubilation of the team.

Both Sheila and Laura watched as the Dutch boat, beginning to make its way to the loading area, caught a freak wake from a chase boat as they'd begun to row. The jar of the sternman's blade being jerked down unexpectedly by the wake wave caused the tiny, light scull to jerk nearly ninety-degrees sideways, drilling directly into the side of the U.S. hull.

Someone screamed as the blue shell was sliced neatly in two and Sheila heard a sharp cry of pain before the back end of the scull quickly disappeared below the surface, taking Sarah with it.

The team watched, standing stiffly silent as Cass struggled to free herself from her shoes. Above the roar of the crowd they could hear the piercing voice of the Irish sculler shouting for Sarah.

"Yank! God damn ya, YANK!!" Cass looked over to see Alanna tearing at her shoes, trying to free herself. The Irish rower caught her eye and pointed into the water.

"She's down there! I think the shell got her leg." Alanna yanked again at her shoes. "God *damn* these bloody things!"

Cass spun and stepped onto the bow of the still-moving Dutch boat as her side of the shell filled with water. The Dutch rower nearest her grabbed her hand, shouting something incomprehensible. Cass yanked her hand free and dove down, following a rapidly fading trail of bubbles. The cool salt water stung as she squinted her eyes open. Above her, she could hear the muffled clanking and rumbling of the motorized launches as they moved to assist in the crash.

Blindly Cass reached ahead, pushing deeper into the blue-black waters. *Sarah! Air, we need... Oh God, where the hell are... wait. WAIT!* Something solid brushed her hand and she turned toward the feeling. Both hands hit something solid...the shell! Cass felt her way along quickly, feeling the broken shell sway as Sarah struggled to free herself.

Desperate hands grabbed at her as Sarah realized someone was down with her. Cass slid her hands down Sarah's leg, grimacing as her fingers found torn flesh. Gritting her teeth at the impulse to scream, the need to open her mouth and gasp for air, she found Sarah's foot, still tied into the mounted shoe and pinned by something solid. *What the hell...pull, no, from the other side, now...PULL.* Putting aside any thought of how this might further injure Sarah, Cass pressed her feet down as hard as she could against the swaying bulk of the shell and pulled forward with her remaining strength.

A muffled pop and a choked cry from Sarah told her they were free. Cass reached forward and grabbed the first soft thing she could find as she felt Sarah go limp beneath her. As tightly as she could, Cass gripped Sarah's racing tunic and kicked for the surface, her vision beginning to go gray around the edges.

Funny, I thought it was supposed to get lighter as we got to the surface.

Back on the dock the U.S. team was frantic, but clearly no one more so than Laura. "*Cass*!" she shouted as Cass disappeared into the water. She was halfway over the rail, her focus on the women beneath surface of the roiling water, when Sheila grabbed her arm.

"Laura. *Laura*!" Sheila yanked the tall rower back to her side of the rail. "They'll have them out of the water by the time you get out there!"

Her face pale with fear, Laura stood gripping the silver railing. "Where the *hell* are the rescue boats? What the *fuck* kind of operation is this?" She sucked in a loud breath and they all watched as finally, *finally* the rescue boats roared up.

"Those idiots will kill them with those propellers!" Pam Collins, Sarah's regular rowing partner and girlfriend, fell against Laura as they watched the rescue divers slip into the water. Instinctively, Laura put her arm around Pam's shoulders. She held her tightly, mindful of the slighter rower's cast and sling. Around her, the other members of the squad were holding each other and their breath as they waited.

"Shush Pammie. Cass will find her." Sheila stood behind the women, a hand on both of their backs.

"Cass will find her."

Laura repeated her assurance, for herself or for Pam, Sheila was not sure. She kept her eyes on the water. *It's been too long, why haven't they...*

"*There they are*!" The shout came from the announcer's booth.

The water turned to foam around her as hands and feet appeared in the water, everyone pulling in every direction. Cass felt Sarah slip from her fingers and she panicked.

"Shh, lovey, it's all right. She's here. Th' medics have got her."

Alanna, the soaking wet Irish rower, pushed her way next to Cass as the emergency team pulled her aboard. "Cass, d'ya hear me? She's out. She's *out*." Finally, Alanna's words penetrated and Cass stopped fighting. The medic next to Alanna nodded her thanks before shoving her aside and placing an oxygen mask on Cass's face.

"Right, then. Yer welcome," Alanna muttered as she watched the medic care for Cass. In the next boat, she could see three or four medical personnel scrambling around the still form of her ex-lover. She was sick at the watery lines of blood she could see dripping off the gunnel over which they'd dragged Sarah's limp body.

"Hang on there and put this on. For shock." She took the thin silvery blanket offered by the other medic and allowed herself to be seated on the small cushions ringing the edge of the deck. The deck tipped sharply as the captain powered his boat toward the emergency docks at the end of the raceway, following the craft carrying Sarah and the other rescuers. Alanna looked back at her own shell, waving once to her still-shocked teammate to let her know she was fine. Then she tipped her head back and began praying that Sarah would be too.

Sheila watched as hands pulled and lifted first Sarah and then Cass out of the water. Pam's gasp as she saw the blood running off Sarah distracted Sheila and she did not see where Cass ended up. She did, however, know she was not going to wait here. Neither, it seemed, was Laura. Grabbing Pam's good hand, Laura began shoving her way back through the crowd.

"Laura, wait!" Sheila's voice stopped her.

Laura snarled as she spun around. "No! Do *not* get in my way!"

Sheila recognized Laura's angry tone for what it was, and let it go. She simply waved her credentials and moved ahead of the two women. "You'll need this *and* me. *Now* let's move."

She was aware that the rest of the team followed them around the end of the raceway to the emergency docking point, but her attention was divided. Laura's face when she had stopped her... Sheila had never seen Laura so...so...*so* what*? So fierce and protective. Hmm, that's new.* Letting that thought go as she worried for her friends, she promised herself she'd visit it again later.

Seven long minutes, three arguments and four threats later, Sheila found herself tucked into a small corner of an outer exam room, waiting with Laura, Pam and Amy for news from inside. She'd kept the rest of the team out, fearing that if there were too many of them in here the medical staff would evict them *all.* From behind the double doors, they could hear sharp voices calling orders, occasionally sounds of running feet and the sharp sound of metal implements hitting the ground. Once in a while, over the top of the other sounds, one clear voice demanded to be heard. Sheila glanced at Laura and raised an eyebrow, smiling at Laura's nod of confirmation.

"She sounds pretty pissed, doesn't she?"

"Yup. I'd say that's a good thing." Laura moved to Sheila's side. "Whaddya think? Can you get in there?"

"Not now. Shit." Sheila ran her fingers through her hair. She was distracted, her attention split between the sounds of the emergency workers in the next room and her own memories of an accident nearly a decade before. Another regatta, another crabbed boat and injured rower. That time the rower had been her friend, Tory and the accident had nearly taken her life, not to mention her leg.

CHAPTER THIRTY-SEVEN

"I'm fine, I'm telling you." Cass pushed away the hands pressing in on her in an effort to breathe. "Would somebody *please* tell me how Sarah is?" She repeated her frustrated demand, just as she had for the last half hour. They had about another ten seconds before she opened up a can of Cass-style whoop-ass on the folks here. *They damned well understand me, they're just pretending not to speak English!* Sucking in a deep breath for one last attempt to find out just what the hell had happened to her teammate, she was startled into coughing by a warm hand on her arm. For once it was not someone poking her or sticking her with a needle.

"Shh, Cass, it's me." Gentle hands eased her up, rubbing her back until the coughing subsided.

Cass slid the oxygen mask off her face and smiled as Amy's

face came into focus. “Hey.” She glanced around at the faces of the medical staff as they muttered and made notations. “Are you here to spring me? Where’s Sarah? How is she? They won’t—”

Amy smiled and continued rubbing Cass’s back. “Whoa there, Nugget. One question at a time. Sarah’s in the other room and they’re checking her out. I snuck in here and they either don’t mind me, or I’m too small to be seen.” The diminutive cox grinned at Cass, then started as a loud cry came from the other room. “Oh God, Cass are you okay?”

“I think so, yeah. I just got a little fuzzy and waterlogged there at the end.” She turned to Amy. “Where’s La—everybody else?”

Amy saw right through her. “*Everybody*, including Laura, is outside, driving the staff nuts. In fact, I should pop out to let them know you’re okay. I thought Laura was going to swim from the docks to get to you.”

Amy cocked her head to the side, considering. She was still surprised by the pain she’d seen on Laura’s face when Cass had disappeared into the water. Another cry from the next room brought her attention back to Cass. “Look, I’m gonna duck out and then back in, if I can. Stay put, be good and they’ll kick you out soon, okay?”

Exhausted, worried about the sounds coming from next door, Cass nodded. She grimaced as Amy slid the oxygen mask back in place. She was glad to see Amy, she just wished Amy were Laura.

Cass felt herself drift and she let her eyes slide shut. *Just for a moment...*

CHAPTER THIRTY-EIGHT

Laura sat huddled in the small plastic chair the orderly had provided, and Sheila was careful not to disturb her as she entered. She quietly moved another chair close to Laura's and turned it so that she could see not only Cass's face but down the hall toward the operating room as well. She had finally gotten someone to give some answers and found that they had taken Sarah into surgery to clean up and repair the damage to her leg. The Dutch shell had broken her fibula and wrought havoc on the muscles of her lower leg. They were waiting to find out the extent of the damage. Sheila had left Amy sitting with Pam and the rest of the team while she'd gone in to give Cass the latest news. She'd found Cass fast asleep, one hand curled into a fist against her pale cheek, and Laura crouched in the only other chair in the room.

It was obvious that Laura cared for Cass. And just as obvious that she was torn about it. And Sheila couldn't afford to have that. Not now.

"Laura," she said softly, careful not to wake Cass. When Laura didn't react, Sheila tried again, louder this time. "Laura, look at me."

Laura looked up, her green eyes haunted.

"I need you here with me right now, Laura."

When Laura spoke, her voice was raspy and uneven. "I'm here, Coach. I swear."

"Then act like it." Sheila's voice was sharper than she'd intended, but her words had the effect for which she'd been looking. Laura sat up straighter and turned to face her, an expression of surprise on her face.

"Sorry, Coach. I was...thinking."

"I could see that. Want to share?" Sheila wanted to be sure, very sure, that Laura's head was in the game.

"I, ah...I pushed her away, you know." She nudged her chin toward Cass.

"When?"

"A few days before the race. Told her we should back off. Take it easy." Laura's voice was low and laced with disgust. "And I realized today that...I was an idiot."

"Yes," Sheila agreed. "You were."

"And I...what?"

Sheila shrugged. "Don't expect me to deny it. You were an idiot to push someone like Cass out of your life. Unless you don't have feelings for her."

"No, I do. That's just it. I was, I mean, we were...then Shelly. And Shelly makes everything..."

"Ugly." Sheila glanced over to make sure their conversation wasn't disturbing Cass. "Sorry, Laura, I know you dated, but the woman's poison."

Laura sighed. She looked from Cass to the still empty hallway that led to the operating room. "I know. I *know*," she repeated. "I...I've wondered for a while just what kind of control she had over Brenda, you know? She, Shelly, she likes control. Needs it. Bren...she was looser. More open. Shelly hated that. They used to fight all the time. That's one of the reasons Bren asked if I would help, you know. It wasn't really for her, but for Shelly. She wanted to know how they could stop. How she could get Shelly to let her...let her live." The last words came out in a broken whisper and then Laura fell silent.

Sheila sat, silently keeping vigil over both women while she processed what she'd heard. She didn't really know what to say and felt out of her depth. Hospital staff moved efficiently along the corridor, but she could see no signs of movement from the doors that led to the operating room. She glanced at her watch; it had been well over an hour since they'd taken Sarah away and she wanted an update.

"She's pretty amazing, isn't she?"

Laura's question startled Sheila, and for a moment she thought Laura was talking about Shelly again. She looked over to find Laura's gaze on Cass's face, her hand resting on the blanket inches from Cass's.

"Yes, she is."

"God, that was amazing today, what they did."

"It was."

"I...I still want to run from this." Laura's voice was so quiet that Sheila had to bend to hear it.

"You'd hurt her if you did."

"I know." Laura's fingers twitched, as if she'd started to reach for Cass's and then had backed off. "Can I tell you something, Coach?"

"Sure."

"I'm afraid. Of this." She looked toward Cass and then back up at Sheila. "But I was more afraid today of losing the chance at this."

"Then," Sheila said, rising silently to her feet, "I think you should focus on that."

Laura nodded and when Cass moaned and twitched in her sleep, she carefully reached up and brushed an errant curl from her forehead. "I think I will. But..." She too stood and moved toward the doorway with Sheila. "I have one or two things I think I need to take care of."

Sheila studied Laura for a long moment. Her face was in

profile, lit from one side by the light spilling into the room from the open door. Her expression, so often haunted and tense, was different now. More open. With a strength in it Sheila hadn't seen for a long time. A very long time. She caught Laura's eye and said softly, "Amy told you what happened before the race?"

"Yes." Laura's voice was firmer.

"And these...things...you have to take care of. Do they involve anyone I know?"

"No one worth mentioning." Laura's eyes had been locked upon the sleeping figure in the bed but suddenly snapped up to meet Sheila's gaze. "Would you stay with her, Coach? I don't want her to be alone. Not now. Not until I...just not now."

"Laura—" Sheila began, only to be cut off.

"It's okay, Sheila. I'm done being an idiot. Now I'm going to be smart about this."

Laura's eyes met hers steadily and finally Sheila nodded, satisfied with what she saw there. She told Laura, "I was going to ask the nurse for an update on Sarah. Can you send her in here on your way out?"

Sheila waited for Laura's nod before stepping back into the room and settling on the chair nearest the bed. She didn't know what Laura had planned, but she certainly didn't want to be near Shelly Michaels anytime soon.

CHAPTER THIRTY-NINE

Shelly tapped a perfectly manicured nail impatiently as she waited for her cameraman. She glanced at her watch, muttering again at how much time they were wasting. Finally, she grabbed her tote and tapped the man's arm.

"Look, I'll meet you at the hospital. I don't have time for this."

She ignored his indifferent shrug as she spun on her heel and headed inside. She was looking forward to getting out of this damnable heat, out of this noisy, smelly place. One more week of racing and she would be gone. She was disappointed her little intrigue hadn't caused more trouble, especially for Laura. It seemed to have done the opposite, in fact, pushing the little snit of a brunette harder. *Damn her and her medal. And damn the producers for wanting me to interview her.* As she pushed her way through the crowd, Shelly began forming the questions she would ask Cass Flynn. If she worded things right, she could probably stir up more trouble for the little rower. It helped that the crew she beat had been the one Shelly had hinted might be tampered with. Lost in her thoughts, she didn't see the woman standing in her way until it was almost too late.

"Going somewhere, Shelly?"

"Yes, as a matter of fact. I'm here to meet with the...hero." Shelly pasted a false smile on her face, aware that they were in a crowded lobby. *Always have to maintain that air of friendly approachability, even when it kills you.*

Laura took Shelly's arm and steered her out of the lobby and down the hall. They came to a stop at an alcove near Cass's room. People passed them, intent on their business.

"I'm going to paraphrase you, Shelly. Stay the hell away from Cass. The network can find someone else to interview her."

"Oh, I don't think so. Why should they?" Shelly stepped away from Laura, staring out the window. "I think a lot of people would like to know more about little Miss Flynn. I'd like to be the one to tell them." She returned to Laura, stepping close. "A lot of people would like to know if the rumors are true too. It's interesting, don't you think, that the boat she beat is the one she's rumored to have tampered with? I find coincidences *so* fascinating, don't you?"

"You're a piece of work. Why don't you just leave her out of this?"

"Because, my love, I'm finding it much more satisfying to fuck with *her*, than I ever did with you. Because when I fuck with her, I *am* fucking with you."

"I know you started the rumors about Cass, that you got that message to the officials."

Shelly shrugged. "So what if it was me? You can't prove it. That's the insidious thing about rumors. They're just little wisps of nothing that can lead to something...or not." She aimed a sharp smile at Laura. "I am really going to enjoy asking the *hero* some questions."

Laura grabbed Shelly's arm as the reporter stepped back into the hall. She tried again.

"Shel. Don't do this."

Shelly shook off Laura's arm. "Fuck you. You can't stop me. If I do my job well enough, maybe they'll end up taking the shiny medal away from your girlfriend. And there's not a thing you can do about it, is there?"

"Maybe she can't, but I think I can," another voice said.

Shelly spun to face the newcomer. Accompanied by a long-legged blond with clear blue eyes, the speaker stepped into Shelly's personal space, forcing Shelly to take a step back. Her retreat pushed her into Laura, who held her firmly in place. Behind both women was Alanna, her blue eyes wide as she watched the scene unfold before her.

Shelly recovered her poise quickly. She set herself belligerently and squared off with the woman who'd invaded her space. "Who the fuck are you?"

"Jane Zimmerman, sportswriter for ESPN Magazine. And wouldn't my publishers and my readers—who, by the way, number more than four times your viewership—be interested in the little tête-à-tête I just overheard?" Zimmerman looked at Laura, then back to Shelly. The blue-eyed blond with her eased her way into the alcove, effectively closing off any escape Shelly might have. Shelly saw her nod briefly to Laura.

"Now, you were saying?" The sportswriter...*Zimmerman*, she recalled...asked her a question.

"I don't know what you're talking about."

"Oh, I think you do. I am fairly certain I overheard you telling this woman that you were involved in implicating a competitor at these Games in something she was, in fact, innocent of. That, and I'm paraphrasing here," she said with a tight smile, "you were going to continue these rumors and try to get her stripped of a medal. How am I doing so far?" Zimmerman pulled out her recorder and powered it on.

Laura nodded in agreement, a small smile playing across her lips. "I think you've got it pretty much right."

Shelly looked from Zimmerman to the tall blond with her, then turned to face Laura. She spun on Zimmerman and pointed toward the room in which Cass was recovering. "You don't know what you're talking about. You don't know what she did."

"No, but *I* know what she didn't do and what *you* did." Alanna's soft lilt was laced with anger. "Isn't it interesting now, that when we inspected our rigging we did find someone had loosened the gates? And, wouldn't you know, when we spoke with that lovely lass from the boathouse she had a great deal to say about who had been visiting late last night."

Alanna ranged herself squarely alongside Laura, and Shelly glared, white-faced and angry, at the women ringing her.

Zimmerman spoke up again. "I also know that I heard you telling this woman how much you liked spreading your crap just to fuck with her. I'm pretty sure that'd make an interesting story for the magazine, don't you agree?"

"Bite me." Shelly shouldered her way between Zimmerman and the still unidentified blond and headed toward the exit, running headlong into her cameraman as he entered. Both ended up on the ground, and Shelly screeched at him, slapping at the hand that he offered to help her get up.

Laura turned to Zimmerman and held out her hand.

"Ms. Zimmerman, thanks a lot."

"No problem and call me Jane." She waved to the woman standing silently nearby, still holding a bright bouquet of flowers. "I believe you've met my partner, Anne," she added drily.

Laura shook hands with Anne, smiling. "You probably don't remember me, Anne, but we've met. At the airport? The day Cass arrived?"

"I don't recall actually meeting you," said Anne, eyeing her carefully.

Laura realized that Anne was remembering the cold shoulder with which she'd treated Cass upon her arrival. She felt a warm flush of embarrassment at her behavior and offered an apology. "I'm sorry, that was a really bad day."

"I also don't remember giving you my cell number?" This time Anne's expression was warmer and Laura could see a hint of a smile playing around her lips.

"Yeah. I, um, well, borrowed Cass's cell phone to call you." She steered the three women back into the alcove. "Cass told me about you, and the magazine your partner works for," she added with a smile toward Jane and then shrugged. "I figured Jane might be able to help."

Jane laughed with the rest. "I'm glad I could. We came as soon as you called, we were really upset about the accident."

"Cass is fine. We're waiting to hear about Sarah." They fell silent for a moment before Laura looked up again. "Oh, I'm sorry. This is Alanna Doyle, of Ireland." Despite the seriousness of the situation she couldn't resist adding, with a smile and nod, "and Olympic silver medalist."

Alanna's bright grin spread across her freckled face as she shook hands all around. "And never a finer medal won, I'd wager."

"Great to meet you. Both of you. Congratulations." Anne smiled at Laura then glanced back down the hallway and shook her head. "We were going to come by to check on Cass later, so I'm really glad you called when you did."

"I'm incredibly glad you did. I didn't know how else I was going to stop her. Your timing was perfect. Did you really overhear everything?"

"Not all of it, just enough to make her think we heard more."

"Nice."

Jane turned to her partner. "Honey, why don't you go on in and visit Cass? I think I'd like to sit out here and chat with Laura and Alanna a bit."

Laura watched as Anne strode down the hall and disappeared into Cass's room. Jane pulled Laura into a nearby seat and settled herself across from Laura while Alanna sat on a nearby bench.

Pulling the small digital recorder from her back pocket again, Jane checked it, then set it on the table before them. She waved toward the device and said, "I have a feeling that Shelly's not finished, so why don't you tell me a story?"

CHAPTER FORTY

Cass rocked back and forth, trying to ease her nerves as she waited for the ceremony to begin. To her left, behind the lowest of three podiums, were the two Dutch rowers, their orange and white track suits blinding in the afternoon sunlight. To the right, behind the second-highest podium were Alanna and Kay, bright in their green and white uniforms. Before Cass and Pam was the tallest of the three podiums, the one onto which they would step in just a few minutes. Sucking in a breath at the flutter of nerves that threatened to overwhelm her, she instead turned and scanned the crowd in the stands, hoping to catch a glimpse of the rest of her team.

"They're over there." Pam nudged her shoulder and pointed further to the left with her good hand.

"Thanks." Cass flicked her gaze over the group of excited

women, grinning as Sheila gave her a thumbs-up. Spotting one of the assistants standing behind a tripod, she turned to Pam and smiled. "Gonna take the tape over to Sarah right after?"

"Yeah." Pam smiled sadly. "She's watching the coverage on TV, but I promised we'd make a tape just for her."

"I so wish she could be here." Cass nervously tugged her team polo straighter. It was unusual to get a medal and not be in her racing unitard. She felt almost awkward in the team shorts and polo.

"Me too." Pam's expression brightened as she continued. "But, the docs say she's doing much better. I wish we could have put this off one more day, then she might have been able to be here."

"At least we get to get our medals the same day the eight get theirs." Cass leaned forward and looked along the row at the twenty-seven women clustered around the end of the docks awaiting their turn, grinning as Amy flashed her a bright thumbs-up from where she stood with the rest of her crew. Behind her stood Laura, and Cass was warmed by the smile she sent her way. The flutter that ran through her echoed the butterflies that had taken root in her stomach, and Cass laughed at herself. She wasn't entirely certain which unsettled her more, the pending medals ceremony or her reaction to the smallest smile from her elusive friend.

A call from the announcer's booth sent a wave of murmuring through the crowd, and Cass assumed they were closer to starting. The officials had postponed the doubles' medal ceremony following the crash and Sarah's injury, but only after an outcry from the International Rowing Federation and several teams in the regatta. The officials had at first demanded that the U.S. put forward representatives to receive the medal, but Coach Adler had flatly refused. Since there were more races to be run, she'd argued, there was no need to rush things and a few days would give at least one team member a chance to be present.

Cass had pushed for an even longer delay so that Sarah could be up there with her, but in the end the U.S. team had been forced to go with Cass and Pam, as Sarah's representative. In the end it was Sarah who'd insisted that they go ahead with the ceremony, and she who had suggested that Pam be her stand-in. So the doubles ceremony had been scheduled for the same day as the eights ceremony.

Just when she thought her nerves couldn't take it anymore, the band played a loud salute, and a man in a deep red jacket strode to the microphone. He held up his hands for quiet and the crowd quickly stilled. The man spoke to the crowd, using the traditional format of speaking first in French, then in English and then in Chinese, the language of the host country.

"Today's ceremony is a special one," he began, his expression solemn. "We honor not only our champions but the dedication and heart that is evidenced in the pursuit of excellence. The athletes who stand before you represent the very best that we can be. Please allow me to introduce, representing the International Rowing Federation, Francois deMarche." The crowd cheered as a distinguished man stepped forward, his dapper suit at odds with the women standing on the podium in their team uniforms.

DeMarche stepped forward and shook the hand of the master of ceremonies. Behind him walked a young woman in a long, white silk dress trimmed in green, carrying a silver platter bearing the Olympic Medals. The wide red silk ribbons fluttered in the breeze as they moved forward onto the medals platform. Another young woman, dressed identically to the first, followed with a tray of flowers and laureates. DeMarche turned and faced the three teams of women and waited for the announcer to begin the ceremony.

"Winner of the Bronze medal, representing the Netherlands, Magda Sondag and Talina Bröeder." The crowd erupted in cheers as the two Dutch rowers stepped onto the podium. DeMarche reached up to lay the ribbon holding the bronze medal over each rower's neck, then he presented them with small bouquets of flowers and shook each woman's hand. They each raised their bundles of flowers and waved to the crowd as they were cheered by their countrymen.

DeMarche passed before the empty center podium and stopped before the one to Cass and Pam's right. Alanna flashed Cass a quick smile as she took Kay's hand and raised it high. The announcer's words were nearly lost as the crowd cheered again. "Winner of the Silver medal, representing the Republic of Ireland, Alanna Doyle and Kay Sinclair." As with the Dutch rowers, deMarche laid the medals around the women's necks and then presented them with their flowers.

Cass and Pam cheered with the rest as the team who'd come so close to beating them raised their bouquets high and saluted the crowd. The noise was almost deafening now, the crowd chanting "USA" as deMarche turned and stepped over to his right, centered exactly in front of the highest platform. His sharp, dark eyes flashed over them both and he shot Cass a ghost of a wink before cocking his head as the announcer spoke once again. "Winner of the Gold medal, representing the United States of America, Cassandra Flynn and Sarah Sullivan! Sarah was, as we all know, injured in an accident following the final race, so her medal will be accepted by her teammate, Pamela Collins."

Pam gripped Cass's hand and gave a sharp tug, pulling her up onto the podium, then she raised their hands high in the air. Cass was overwhelmed with emotion and couldn't fight the swell of tears. She was glad Pam had taken the lead and pulled her up, for a second she was afraid her legs wouldn't hold her. As the announcer repeated his words in French and Chinese, she fought to get hold of her emotions. It all seemed so surreal.

So...magical.

She was standing on a podium at the Olympic games. And not just any podium, but the *highest* podium. Any second the representative of her sport's international federation was going to place around her neck a gold medal. Pam squeezed her hand again and Cass looked over at her.

"Okay?" Pam whispered as deMarche stepped forward.

Cass just nodded as Pam freed her fingers. She bent low, ducking her head as his arms came up and the weight of the medal settled around her neck.

Over the noise of the crowd and the cheering of her teammates, she heard him say in his heavily-accented English, "Congratulations, young lady."

Reaching up, she brushed her fingers over the shining, surprisingly heavy medal and then met deMarche's gaze. "Thank you," she choked out. She watched as Pam leaned down to accept the medal from him and saw that she was just as overwhelmed. DeMarche reached behind him and Cass bent low again, this time to receive a crown of laurel leaves, the traditional Greek symbol of the champion. He then handed her a large bouquet of flowers, and then turned and repeated the same pattern with Pam. After exchanging kisses on each cheek and shaking hands with them both, he turned and led the two silk-clad women off to one side.

Cass, still in something of a daze, reached down to lift the surprisingly heavy medal from her chest. It was, of course, upside down, but it was still easy to make out the graceful winged goddess of victory as she strode through the stylized amphitheater, the Parthenon etched in the background. Curving around the top were the words "XXIV Olympiad Beijing 2008." Her hand shaking, Cass rubbed her fingers over the wide band of white jade on the back, feeling the Olympic rings engraved on the golden center.

Any second now I will wake up and this will all be a— Even as she thought it, the first strains of her own national anthem began to play and suddenly Cass snapped back into the present. She lifted her chin as she and Pam turned toward the flagpole. There, at the base, the flag began to unfurl as the red-clad soldiers lifted it into the position of honor. Her throat tightened and she didn't bother to blink back tears as the anthem played. Nor did she try to sing. She lifted her hand, medal still held tightly in her fingers, over her heart and just mouthed the words, suffused with joy and pride as the flag climbed the pole, flanked by the bright colors of Ireland and the Netherlands.

After all the pain, all the rejection and hardship, she was here.

A million images flashed in her memory. Of her uncle, his face red and mottled as he shouted at her, telling her that she was as useless as her mother. Her aunt's tight little mouth as she belittled Cass's every hope and dream. Her cousins' cruel taunts and mean games. The pitying face of the nurse when she'd awakened in the hospital, her leg and back nothing but a seething morass of pain. The therapist who told her she'd never row again.

After...everything...everyone...she was here.

She'd won. Nothing and nobody could ever take that away from her.

As the last strains of music faded, the crowd again cheered, and this time it was Cass who seized Pam's hand and raised it high. They waved to the crowd again and then turned to bring the other two teams up on top of the podium with them. Alanna wrapped an arm around Cass's shoulders, her wide, open face alight with happiness.

"Well done to you! Well done to you both!"

Cass gave her a hug. "And to you, and Kay," she added smiling again at Alanna's rowing partner. The six of them posed for photographs and Cass made sure that the assistant coach with the video camera for Sarah got a good shot of them all before she jumped off the podium.

She and Pam stepped over to meet their team and were immediately enveloped by the girls. Their reunion was cut short, however, as the master of ceremonies was waving forward the larger crowd of eights teams. Just as Cass spotted Laura, the steward started lining the women up to file out in procession. Laura reached out, but was pulled back into position by another steward.

"Go," Cass said as the steward waved them forward again. "I'll catch up with you after."

Laura managed to break free long enough to lean forward and whisper, "I'm *so* proud of you!" before being pulled along with her team to stand behind their second-place podium.

Cass let herself be shuffled backward as the medals ceremony was repeated for the eights. She cheered and clapped as Amy led her crew up onto the second-highest podium to received their well-deserved silver medal. She only had eyes for one woman. Cass watched as Laura bent low to receive her award, then as she stood, her hand wrapped around the medal on her chest. Laura did as she had—lifted the metal disk and examined it, turning it over in her hand, almost as if she were weighing it. She seemed to blow out a breath and then look up and out, her eyes searching the crowd. Cass held her breath and then stilled as Laura's eyes flicked over to where she stood and then stopped, her gaze locked on Cass, her green eyes bright with tears.

In that instant, Cass was lost. Her heart skipped and her stomach dropped. It took everything she had not to break through the line of volunteers, step onto the podium, and wrap her arms around Laura. She wanted to celebrate with her, to commiserate over the final ten strokes of the eights race, and to celebrate their shared victories.

And she wanted more.

Her own words came back to her. "*I guess I've just never, you know. Been in love.*"

Sending Laura a wide-open smile, Cass thought, *I guess I can't say that anymore, can I?* That thought was followed quickly by another.

Now what do I do?

CHAPTER FORTY-ONE

The milling crowd around her was maddening. Immediately after the medals were presented to the eights, the media had crowded in, pulling the women in different directions, and Cass had lost sight of Laura. Adding to the bedlam was the impromptu party that seemed to spring up following all of the medal ceremonies at these games. Music would start, Cass was never sure who would start it, and then the party would begin. Everyone, it seemed, would dance. If nothing else, Cass had learned that the Chinese, especially the younger generation, loved their music and loved to move. This ceremony, the second to last of the rowing events, seemed to have brought out a larger than normal crowd and she realized that this was just the beginning of a much larger party.

"Hey, what's going on? Oh, did you hear?" Amy bounced

over to Cass and looped her arm through hers. She reached out and brushed her fingers over the gold medal around Cass's neck, and then lifted her own silver medal. "Gosh, they're pretty, aren't they?"

Shaking her head, Cass tried to sort through Amy's rapid-fire and confusing questions. "Hear what? And yes...they're stunning." She bent to look at Amy's silver. The jade on the back of the silver medal was green, in contrast to the white on the gold medal, but the weight of each was just the same. And, she was sure, meant just as much to Amy.

"Hmm?" Amy was holding both medals in her hands. She looked up and grinned. "Oh, rumor has it that the, ah...bitch reporter was canned today."

"What happened?" For the first time, Cass realized that the ever-intrusive Shelly Michaels was nowhere to be seen, and she could usually be found in the thick of any media event. Thinking back, Cass realized she hadn't seen Shelly at all since... "Huh. I haven't seen her since just before our race."

"Yeah." Amy leaned closer. "Rumor has it she stopped by the hospital. She was trying to get an *exclusive*." Amy made air quotes to emphasize her point. "She was stopped at the door."

"No way."

"Yup. Laura got right up in her face and so did a few others. Then I heard that Laura made some calls, more people showed up, and...well, the bitch is on the street!" Amy clapped her hands and grinned again. "Couldn't have happened to a nicer person, though I kind of wish they'd stopped in the psych ward to up her meds."

"Yeah," Cass agreed faintly. She couldn't believe it. "Laura did that?" She asked, trying to keep her voice level.

"Yeah. Karen," she said, referring to one of the team's assistant coaches, "said that Laura was *fierce*. She halfway expected to hear her growl. Wish I could have seen it."

"Me too." Cass tried again to spot Laura in the crowd.

"Have you had a chance to talk to her yet?"

Cass shook her head. "No, I...wait, there she is." Less than five feet from her, weaving through the dancing fans and athletes, was Laura. Cass caught her breath slightly as a bright camera light paused for a moment on Laura and the rest of her teammates.

Amy laughed and nudged her, "C'mon, Cass, what happened between you two? She never left your side that night in the hospital."

"Yeah, that's what Coach said." Cass frowned slightly. "But after that...nothing. Well, mostly nothing. I thought we...but I guess it was just me. Or this..." Cass waved her arm at the show surrounding them. She shrugged and gave Amy a halfhearted smile. "It's okay. I just hoped—" Embarrassed, Cass ducked her head and looked away from Amy, inadvertently right at Laura. Another camera crew's light danced over the crowd again, haloing Laura's red hair, made more brilliant by the contrasting intermittent flashes of camera flashes. "God, she's gorgeous," Cass breathed.

Delighted, Amy laughed and nudged Cass. "I *knew* it! Come on, just go *talk* to her."

Embarrassed at having voiced her thought, Cass shook her head. "No, she wouldn't...I mean, I..." She did not really know how to explain to Amy what had happened. What had they shared, really? One amazing hug? A few hours of feeling of being connected in the rarefied atmosphere of the Olympics? A note? She thought there was something, but the mess with Shelly, the racing, the accident and then...nothing.

Cass had awakened in the exam room to find Coach leaving her clean clothes. Sheila had filled her in on Sarah's condition and was waiting to drive Cass back to their quarters in the village. When she'd arrived, everyone had been concerned, solicitous, but the one face Cass had wanted to see was nowhere to be found. The common room had been returned to normal during her overnight stay in the hospital, the maintenance team having finally gotten around to fixing the dysfunctional air conditioning. The days after were filled with a whirlwind of racing heats for the other events, visits to Sarah in the hospital and nights of restless, exhausted sleep. Cass knew Laura was avoiding her but she had thought they were past that.

After getting the all-clear from the medical center, she'd looked for Laura every free minute, which had not been a lot.

When Laura was off the water, after tuning for her race, Cass was in an interview. When she was in the gym, Laura was not. Finally, it got to be so obvious that Laura was avoiding her that she'd simply stopped looking. As much as she'd wanted to push, however, she also wanted to honor Sheila's request to not get into things until after the races. She, too, knew how important it was to stay focused, so she'd stayed away.

Determined to enjoy her last days in Beijing, she'd watched the final heats along with Anne Landers, and her partner, Jane. Her heart ached to think that Laura had been at the hospital but not stayed to visit her when she was awake. Anne and Jane had celebrated with her team when Laura's eight won the silver medal yesterday and both women promised to keep in touch with Cass after they returned home.

It was frustrating and she decided that tonight she would simply corner Laura and ask her what was up. *Hey, it worked once before. You called her on her rudeness and she...what Cass? Opened up? Yeah, for about three weeks, then bam! Disappearing Laura. Crap. I don't know what to do. I just know that I...*

Spotting Laura again in the churning crowd, Cass decided it was worth one last shot. "You know what, Amy? You're right. Let's go." She began to thread her way through the undulating crowd, Amy trailing along behind. Cass came to such an abrupt halt that Amy, still dancing, slammed into her.

"Hey!" Amy ducked under Cass's arm to peer around her and then swore softly.

Cass felt her heart plummet as the strapping captain of the Australian women's team swept Laura into a breathtaking, heart-stopping kiss. Cass spun away, her determination to talk to Laura waning. "I, uh, think it's a moot point anyway." Cass gave Amy a weak smile and headed back to where they had been before.

"Oh damn, Cass. I didn't know..." Amy trailed off, and glanced back to where Laura was disentangling herself from Abby and glancing quickly around. That did not look like a woman in love. At least not in love with the person doing the kissing. Amy checked on Cass and saw that she was heading toward the edge of the athletes' area. She turned again toward Laura and squared her shoulders. Time to find out what the hell was going on.

Several feet away, Laura pulled herself out of the unexpected embrace. Amy arrived in time to hear her mutter, "Abby!" She slapped the solid arm of the woman who'd accosted her. "What the hell are you doing?"

Abby grinned unrepentantly and gave her friend a last smacking kiss on the lips and this time, Amy noted with satisfaction, Laura actually winced. "Relax, mate, just saying hello!" Abby linked her arm with Laura's, letting the music carry their movements for a moment as she watched her friend search the crowd. "Who're ya looking for?"

Laura returned her old college roommate's grin and dipped her head to the left. Abby followed her gaze, and then shook her head. "Uh, Laura, darlin,' you'll have to help me here, there're a million lovely lasses over there."

"Her, the little brunette."

Amy watched Abby scan the cluster of women again before her eyes landed on Cass, who was at the moment enveloped in Big John Sullivan's arms. Apparently they'd let the families enter the area now, and Mr. and Mrs. Sullivan, always popular with the team, had been dragged into the dancing with the U.S. squad.

"Ah...the one that big bloke's holding tightly to?" Abby chuckled as Laura whipped her head around.

Amy spoke up from behind them. "That's no bloke, that's Sarah's dad, John Sullivan."

Suddenly serious, Abby smiled a hello at Amy but asked, "How *is* Sarah? That was bloody awful, that crash."

Amy smiled up at Abby and then squeezed Laura's arm, casually sliding between the two women as she joined them. "Sarah's good, she's going to be fine, according to the docs." Giving Laura's arm another squeeze she said, "Hey, Abby, I'm gonna steal Laura, okay?"

Giving Laura a last hug, Abby pushed her off toward where the U.S. team was gathered. "No worries, I'm off to cause a bit of mischief. Call me when you get home, eh?"

"Will do," said Laura as Amy dragged her away.

"'Ever-Ready Abby,' Laura? What the hell's up with that?" Amy pulled Laura through the growing crowd, hoping to spot Cass near the team.

"Hey, she grabbed *me.*" Laura glanced back over her shoulder. "Thanks for the rescue."

"I didn't see you fighting her off." Amy paused, then added, "Neither did Cass."

"Cass...oh crap. Did she see—"

"Yeah, and...dammit, Laura. You should have seen her face!"

"Crap," Laura repeated, then scanned the crowd around them. "Where is she?"

Shrugging, Amy pushed through a groups of excited Dutch rowers. "I don't know. I'm gonna head over that way," she said, pointing. "You try over there. Call me if you find her so I'm not doing this all night."

"Got it. And Amy?" Laura tugged Amy back. "Thanks. You're a good friend."

Amy just grinned and waved as she moved around the back of where the U.S. team was laughing and taking photos. Maybe she'd get lucky and spot Cass here. Or better yet, maybe Laura would get lucky...all around.

CHAPTER FORTY-TWO

Edging around a group of Irish and Swiss team members, Cass spotted Sheila near the media booth. As much as she didn't want to go near the cameras, Cass wanted a moment with her coach. More, she wanted an escape. She stepped into Sheila's line of sight and waited until the bright light of the camera snapped off before stepping forward.

"Coach?"

Sheila smiled and wrapped an arm around Cass's shoulders, steering them both away from the cameras. "Hey." She nodded toward the medal. "Great job, you know. I know I said it before, but..."

Cass lifted a hand to the disc and then looked up at Sheila. "Thanks. And...*thanks*, you know? I, literally, wouldn't have this if you hadn't—"

Sheila stopped them both at the edge of the crowd. "Cass, you are a terrific athlete and a welcome member of our team. I am never happy when a team member is injured, but I will be forever grateful that it was you we called."

Cass could only nod as she fought to keep her voice steady. "I...you'll never know Coach, just how much it meant to me that you included me on the team."

"I have some idea." Sheila wrapped her arms around Cass and gave her a hug. "So, what'd you need to see me for?"

Swallowing, Cass struggled for words. "I...can I get someone to take me back?"

"Are you okay?" Sheila tipped her head and looked closer.

"Yeah…" Cass offered a weak smile. She was overwhelmed, really. First the ceremony, then watching Laura get her medal and realizing just how much she wanted to celebrate with her. Just with her. To share in their success together. To share more than that. She wanted her in ways she'd never wanted anyone, and then to see her wrapped in someone else's arms... Despite her determination, Cass's eyes filled with tears.

"Cass, what's going on?"

Gritting her teeth, Cass just shook her head. This was her problem, her issue. On a day when she should be celebrating her highest achievement, she wanted nothing more than to curl up in her bed and cry. She felt as if her heart were breaking. She couldn't get the image of Laura wrapped in the other woman's arms out of her head. How could she have been so stupid? So naíve?

"Cass." Sheila's voice was soft, and she looked up to see that Sheila had led her around the back of the stands to where the vans waited. "Talk to me. What's going on?"

"I...it's okay, Coach. I'm just...overwhelmed, I think." She lifted her head and met Sheila's gaze steadily, hoping to convince her coach that she was good.

After a moment Sheila nodded. "I'll hunt up Karen and have her run you back. Wait here."

Sheila strode off, leaving Cass alone by the team van. She dipped her head and then slowly lifted the shining medal off her neck. Running her fingers along the finely woven red silk ribbon, she took a moment to steady herself. *Get a grip, Cass. You've got a gold medal. You are not just an Olympian, but an Olympic champion.* Closing her eyes, she let herself remember that shining moment when she and Sarah realized that they'd won. The thrill that had run through her. A thrill matched only by—

"Cass?"

Eyes still closed, Cass froze. The one person she'd wanted to see most in the world only a short time ago...the one person now she was trying desperately to get away from. She felt Laura move closer and held her breath, some vestige of childish determination filling her, telling her that if she didn't open her eyes, didn't breathe, Laura wouldn't see her. She wouldn't have to look up into those depthless green eyes.

A warm hand settled on her forearm and the illusion was shattered. Cass blinked and then forced a small smile. "Oh, hey! Uh, Laura." She glanced past Laura, hoping that the tall Australian wasn't anywhere nearby.

Laura chuckled, her smile cautious. "Yeah. Laura Kelley. Remember me? I picked you up at the airport? Was rude to you?" Laura glanced around, then down again at Cass. "We shared a hug a week or so back? Ring a bell?" Laura turned and looked over her shoulder, then back at Cass. "Who're you looking for?"

"Um, nobody." Flustered, she looked anywhere but at Laura's face. "I'm sorry, it's just that, well..." Cass stopped and looked away. "I haven't seen you, you even moved your bed back to your room, and..." Cass trailed off uncertainly, suddenly angry with herself. She sounded like a sad little girl and hated that. Determinedly, she took a deep breath and for the first time, looked directly into Laura's eyes. "I, um, got your note." At Laura's look of confusion, she explained. "That day, the day of the race. I got your note. It meant a lot to me."

"I'm glad."

Laura stepped closer and Cass's heart stuttered. She looked again over Laura's shoulder, this time desperately hoping to spot Sheila. She was afraid her feelings were there for all the world to see and she needed to get away. Desperate to sound normal, she searched for something, anything to say. "I wanted to...

well, we haven't had five minutes together and I wanted to say congratulations on your win."

"Thanks." Laura looked away and then back again. She gestured vaguely over her shoulder and said, "Listen. About, uh, Abby—"

"Oh, was that her name?" Cass asked hastily, thankful for the growing darkness that hid her rising flush. "Yeah. I'm sorry, I'm sure you want to get back to her. Anyway, uh, well, great job. I'll see you around." She turned and quickly stepped away from the van. She'd find another way back. "Hey!" Cass stopped and looked back at the sound of Laura's voice. The announcer was saying something to the crowd on the waterfront and Cass wasn't certain Laura had spoken.

"Hey," Laura said again, this time in a softer voice as she strode over to where Cass stood. "What's going on?"

"What do you mean?"

"I mean—" She stopped and then simply tilted her head and gazed at Cass, her expression imploring. After a long moment she ran a frustrated hand through her hair and then shrugged, clearly at a loss for words.

Cass tried not to notice that the light hit those auburn curls and made them glow. She tightened her fingers into fists as, against her will, the memory of how soft those curls were flashed across her mind. She watched Laura struggle for words and then realized the absurdity of the moment. She'd spent weeks getting to know this woman, falling for her when she should have been focused on her own preparations. Then she'd been depressed beyond all logical reason the past couple of days when it became clear that Laura was avoiding her. And now here she was, in front of her, and Cass's first instinct was to run away.

Laura shoved her hands into the pockets of her shorts. She peered at Cass and then said, "Cass, I...I want you to know that I want this. But I'm...I need a little time. Can you give me that?"

For the third time that evening Cass felt her heart stutter to a halt. Felt the sickening swoop in her belly and felt a warmth wash over her. "You want...what, Laura?" After the emotional roller-coaster of the past few weeks, she needed to hear it out loud.

Laura frowned and then shifted, her shoulders hunched. She reminded Cass of a teenager about to be punished. After a moment, Laura looked up. "I didn't imagine it, did I? I thought we... I felt like we connected, Cass. I want...I *really* want to explore that. But..." She trailed off and her gaze dropped to the medal hanging once again around Cass's neck. She looked from the gold to the silver around her own neck and blew out a slow breath. "I don't know how to...to get past it."

"What?" Cass couldn't help herself. When Laura hurt, *she* hurt, and she had to do something about that. Couldn't *not* do something. Laying a hand on Laura's arm, she gave it a little shake. "Get past what?"

"I cost us the gold." She whispered, her voice awash in pain. "We... if we hadn't had to do the repechage. Because of Shelly and her goddamned interference, we had to race a *third* race. And...God, it kills me. We had to race again and it was too much. You almost lost your chance too. Because of me. Of...*her*."

"Laura, you can't...you aren't responsible for this, you know." Cass grasped Laura's silver medal and gave it a tug. "Or, I guess, you are. You and your crew just won a silver medal! How can that mean failure?" Dropping the medal, Cass stepped back. "God, you expect so *much* from yourself. You're not responsible for the world, you know. Just you."

Taking a deep breath, Cass plunged on, knowing that she might be pushing too far. "You have to learn how to let this stuff go, Laura, or...I don't know the 'or,' but...you just have to. You are not responsible for any of it. Brenda's death, and God knows it was tragic, was not your fault. Your shell's sabotage, the hearing about me, none of it was *you*. Having met...Shelly," and Cass couldn't keep the anger and revulsion she felt from her voice, "I'm amazed that you're as whole as you are. Look at her! She's damaged, Laura, and she's damaging you. Everything she touches is blackened by...oh, I'm sure evil is too strong a word, but the woman is unbalanced. And you're letting her unbalance you, even now."

Laura turned her stricken gaze to Cass and it took everything in her to not reach forward and wrap Laura in her arms. As much as she wanted to, she wouldn't. Laura had asked for time, and, as much as she wanted what *she* wanted now, she had to step back. Give Laura what she needed. She reached up and laid a gentle hand on Laura's face, her thumb gently caressing her cheekbone, her fingers sliding back into the silken auburn hair. "Please don't get me wrong. I want to explore what we might have too. But... you need to be sure of what you want. *I* need you to be sure."

Cass took a deep breath and stepped back, her hand dropping from Laura's warm skin. She immediately felt the loss and her fingers tingled from the touch. "You asked for time. Okay... When you're ready, come find me."

It took everything she had to turn and walk away, knowing she was leaving Laura in pain.

CHAPTER FORTY-THREE

Cass spun around, letting the almost primal rhythm of the drums carry her where they would through the crowd. Around her, in the flickering semidarkness of the stadium, thousands of other athletes were dancing, swaying, shouting and singing to the music. Cass knew most of those around her couldn't understand a word of what the singers were saying, but right here, right now, the words did not matter. Their spirits were singing. Rejoicing really, in the moment; reveling in the freedom and the high of the post-adrenaline rush that follows the Olympic Games.

Flashes of red, green, gold and black and every shade in between danced past them as smiling athletes bumped and jostled each other in their celebration of a Games well ended. Oh, there had been moments. Profound moments, sad moments, even outrageous moments over the last seventeen days. But, when all was said and done, those moments were now forever lost in time, left to verbose commentators to wax philosophical over in their wrap-up commentary.

By her side, gyrating madly to the music, was Amy. Arms waving, hair flying as if she did not have a care in the world, Amy danced as if her feet were on fire. The drummers' cadence increased, as did the frenzy of movement around her, bringing her back to her surroundings. Cass briefly lost sight of Amy in the undulating crowd, but could see the other members of the U.S. team around her. Faces she was coming to know and some she'd still like to know better.

"This is *amazing*!" Amy's breathless laughter was contagious.

"Yeah."

Cass smiled as she worked her way toward the entrance, peripherally aware that once again, the rhythm of the music changed. Reaching their highest peak yet, the drums suddenly stopped, seeming to take with them the lights from the stadium. Plunged into total blackness, the athletes-turned-dancers stopped and conversations became hushed. Cass felt people moving past her in the ever-fluid ebb and flow of the ocean of athletes on the floor, but heard no voices she recognized; nor, now that she could distinguish one from another, any language that she knew.

For a moment, she felt utterly alone in the teeming throng. She closed her eyes, trying to erase the image of Laura standing before her just a week ago. Alone and so sad. But she'd asked for time and Cass had given it to her. She wished, however, that she knew how much time Laura had meant. *Let it go, Cass. It was the moment. The time you mistook the warm-fuzzy Olympic love for the real thing and now look at you. Crap. This sucks.* She determinedly shook off her bad mood and instead thought of the gold medal Coach had safely tucked away for her. *I did that. I won a gold medal.* For a moment, despite her sadness and confusion, she let herself feel that thrill again.

Lights flooded the stadium floor once more and Cass, along with everyone else, threw their hands up to shield their eyes, reminding Cass of a scene from the *X-Files.* With the drama and spectacle evidenced by the Chinese planning commission, she half expected to see a triangular spaceship floating overhead. Instead the blazing lights danced around the stadium and then swiveled to focus on the main stage once more.

"Cassandra Flynn?" A soft voice called Cass's name.

Cass turned toward the voice, not recognizing the tiny woman with the Korean flag stitched above the Olympic logo on her polo shirt. She did, however, recognize the universal gesture for "picture."

"You want me to take a picture of you?"

The woman smiled and shook her head. "Yes, please. Take picture with you? Yes?"

Surprised, Cass could only nod. "Uh, sure! What's your name?"

The Korean bowed slightly to her while handing her little camera off to her friend. "Xiao Li Ju."

Cass stepped in, throwing her arm around the smaller woman's shoulder. "Uh, well, nice to meet you...Xiao?"

The Korean woman blinked the flash spots out of her eyes and grinned at Cass. "No, no, Cassandra, it is Li Ju." She hesitated for a second and continued, "My friends say only Li." She nodded to Cass. "So, Li? Yes?"

"Oh! Yes, Li!" Cass bowed slightly, smiling at the grin that blossomed on Li's face. "Li it is, and *my* friends call me Cass." She quickly pulled her camera out of her pocket and, gesturing with it to Li and her friend asked, "May I?"

Li and her companion grinned and nodded, moving closely together. Cass pointed the camera and stopped suddenly. "Wait." She grabbed the arm of a passing athlete and shoved the camera in his hands. Li quickly did the same with hers. "Hey, picture?"

The big man grinned, his red-green-and-black cap slipping down to cover one ear. "Yah, mon, no problem."

Cass quickly jumped to stand near the two Korean women, who in turn moved to make room for her in the middle. Cass laughed briefly. She suddenly felt very tall; her five-foot, three-inch muscular frame made her feel as if she towered over her two counterparts. She nodded to her newly elected photographer and he grinned from behind the camera.

"Nice, yes, very nice...okay? Ready...and..." Blinded by the flashes as he quickly took two pictures, Cass could only blink and smile at him as he returned their cameras. She turned back to the women. "Thank you both. I'm sorry, I don't recognize you, are you scullers?" She didn't think so, but perhaps they were reserves on the Korean team.

Li smiled. "No, gymnasts. We, Shinyong and I, saw your races and we wanted to meet you." Both women bowed and smiled again, and Li offered shyly, "You fought well, for your victory."

Cass grinned back and offered a little bow of her own. "Well, thank you, it was great to meet you." She watched the two women disappear into the crowd, chattering happily to each other and peering at Li's camera. Beyond them, she thought she spied the entrance marker and began to move in that direction. The lights of the stadium flickered, then just as suddenly as before, the lights went out. Again.

Cass grumbled to herself, good-naturedly, *Well, how the heck are we supposed to find anything if they keep turning off the lights?* Tonight had been indescribable. So much to see and do, it was all a bit overwhelming. Cass hoped she never lost the wonder and magic of the moment, nor the memory. Despite the lingering sadness over the loss of whatever-it-was she might have had with Laura and the shadow cast by Shelly, Cass had had an amazing experience here.

She was glad she and Amy had left the village before everyone else, just to get some more touring in before the closing ceremonies and Amy's flight later tonight. Since the team didn't have to report for prep for the upcoming Worlds until the first week of September, Cass was not due to fly back to the U.S. until the following week.

Originally, she and a few other scullers had planned to tour parts of China together, but those plans had fallen apart after Sarah's injury. Cass shuddered in the darkness as she relived hearing the grinding, snapping crunch as the Dutch shell cut through the center of theirs just past the finish of their race. She could still taste her fear, feel her frustration as her fingers fumbled to free her feet from the shoes bolted into the foot stretcher and most of all she could hear Sarah's screams as the saltwater rushed in and filled the gaping hole in her leg and thigh. The fine and punishment of the camera boat for causing the Dutch crew to crab at the finish couldn't make up for Sarah's injury, or the long moments spent in the water waiting for the support boats to help her, but the money would go a long way toward Sarah getting good treatment. Pam had wanted to get her back to the States as soon as she could to have an orthopedist look at the injury, but Sarah had insisted on staying through tonight, where she could watch the events live on television. She'd sent her parents down to represent her, to the delight of her dad.

Cass shivered again and resolutely pushed the memory aside, not wanting to think about Sarah or her injury. The possibility that Sarah might not get to row again was unthinkable, though not unimaginable. Not too long ago that prospect had loomed large on her own horizon. It wasn't fair and it sickened Cass to think of it. Sarah had been her mentor, the first person—after Amy—to welcome Cass to the U.S. rowing team's little circle. Now, with Sarah and Pam going home early and a little under a week left to play with, Cass found herself planning on touring China alone. For just a moment, the shouting and laughter among her fellow athletes was overwhelming. She was tired of being alone.

A gasp went up among the athletes, pulling Cass's attention back to crowd, as the stands lit up with ten thousand flickering lights. For the first time since they'd poured onto the floor of the arena, the athletes grew quiet. Cass instinctively turned back toward the way she'd come, wondering what was in store for them now.

"Um, hello." A soft voice said the words in her ear and Cass couldn't help but jump in surprise. Laura had appeared by her side just as little fairy lights began to light up the stadium, appearing intermittently, like stars in the night sky.

Speechless, Cass could only stare up at her. She was the last person she'd expected to find standing next to her, also staring in wonder at the thousands of flickering lights dancing across the velvety blackness of the stadium walls.

Laura nodded in the direction the two Korean women had gone. "Looks like you have some fans."

Heart racing, Cass could only nod. Realizing she had to say something, she stammered, "H-hi. Um..." *Well done, O Smooth One. She finally shows up and you're unable to speak.* "Uh, yeah, they were really sweet." She eyed Laura, searching her face for some clue as to how she was feeling. Her eyes were clear and the tight set of her shoulders—so familiar to Cass—was gone. She seemed...looser, somehow. Lighter. Even as she studied her, however, Laura's expression tightened. She took a half step back from Cass, as if uncertain of her welcome.

Cass felt like an idiot. Here was her opportunity. *She came looking for you, dummy. After a week of no contact, she's here. Say something. Anything!* They stood staring at one another in silence as the music started again, this time a soothing, almost water-like flow to it. A high, lilting voice carried over the crowd, rising and falling perfectly in time with the waves of fairy lights cascading around them. Cass felt for a moment as if she were drowning, but she wasn't panicked. Wasn't afraid. She gazed into Laura's eyes and felt...comforted. Safe. She tilted her head and arched an eyebrow as she offered, softly, "I've missed you."

A quirk of a smile crossed Laura's lips and she moved a tiny bit closer. "Me too. You, I mean." She reached up and massaged the back of her neck, looking around at the milling, chattering crowd, then again up to the stands filled with tiny white lights. When she looked back at Cass her expression was warm, open. "I wanted to...to thank you."

Oh. Her heart sank and she forced a friendly, interested smile across her lips.

"To...thank me?" Cass asked, keeping her voice steady. "For?"

"For not...I don't know. Not pushing me last week. Or maybe *for* pushing me. You were right. I needed to talk to someone. And," she sighed, her next words barely audible in the growing noise of the crowd. "I needed to learn to...let go."

"And have you?" Cass moved closer as the crowd pressed in.

"I'm getting there."

"Do you still need time?"

"Yes, but." Laura held her gaze. "I don't think I need to do it all alone."

Oh, she thought again, but this time instead of her heart sinking to her shoes she felt it rise up, straight through her body, warming her from head to toe. This time she didn't have to force a smile, it came easily. She grinned up at Laura and felt a thrill when she grinned back, no reservations in her expression, those enticing green eyes sparkling.

How long they stood grinning at each other, she had no idea, and she really didn't know what to do next. Then, suddenly flashing back to the evening in the elevator, she reached out and grasped Laura's arm. "Hey, can we start over? I think I'm a bit overwhelmed by, uh, it all." Cass stuck out her hand, "Hi, I'm Cass Flynn, and I'm a huge fan of yours."

Laura gently took Cass's hand in hers, giving her fingers a gentle squeeze. "Laura Kelley, and I have to admit to being a bit of a fan of yours as well."

"Really?" Cass couldn't help but be aware of the small quaver in her voice, despite her best effort. She also was aware that she was still holding Laura's hand.

"Really." Laura kept hold of Cass, and Cass tried not to focus on how much she enjoyed the fit of the other woman's hand around hers.

"I've been wanting to talk to you for days, you know. But with the regatta and all...what I mean is, I had to work through some things and to think..." Laura trailed off, as if suddenly unsure of herself. "And when I finally got to a place where I *could* talk to you, I couldn't find you."

Cass blew out a long breath as she processed Laura's words. She struggled to find the right thing to say, afraid that if she said the wrong thing, Laura would disappear again. Something about the nature of her relationship with Laura threw her, kept her off balance, and not in a good way. She was sick of that feeling. That would change tonight, she decided; she was letting the injured Cass go and reclaiming what was hers—the Cass who could do anything. Lifting her eyes to Laura's, she decided the direct approach was the best. "I'm glad you found me. But," and she hated to ask this, but for her own well-being she knew she needed to, "are you going to run away again? 'Cause I hate that, you know."

Laura studied her for a moment, then leaned closer, her voice intense. "Cass. I meant what I said in that note. That I wanted to talk. About...well, about us. I...I like what we had between us. I thought it was good."

Cass nodded, caught by the intensity of Laura's gaze. Here, in an arena of thousands, she felt as if it were just the two of them alone. "It was. But," she swallowed and looked away. "You hurt me. You...you didn't come to see me. At least, not when I could see you."

"I know." Laura closed her eyes and then whispered, "I'm sorry. I thought I needed to be away from you to make things better, and it just ended up making things worse."

"Did Amy give you my message before your last race?"

Laura's eyes popped open in surprise. "No." Then she frowned and thought for a moment. "Wait, just before she climbed into the boat she gave me a hug and she never does that." She smiled down at Cass. "That was you?"

"Yeah. It was the same message I sent before your repechage."

"I'm beginning to like your messages, though I'd like to get them firsthand."

Cass returned Laura's smile with a bright one of her own, her heart soaring. "If we're having a do-over, I think that can be arranged." They stood silently for a moment, looking anywhere but at each other as the next act came on the massive stage behind them, but standing near enough that their arms brushed.

Around them, the crowd moved and muttered as the final speakers paid tribute to the athletes. The Olympic flag was handed off to the representative from London with all the pomp and splendor that could be mustered, an adorable little Chinese girl enchanted the crowd and athletes with her song, and the lights continued to dance across the arena floor.

For the next two hours, Cass and Laura enjoyed the show, with Cass conscious of every movement Laura made. They laughed and chatted about everything and nothing and cautiously rekindled the friendship that had grown between them over the course of the Games. In the press of the crowd, they shared the wonder, noise and excitement of the final, official hours of the Olympic Games...along with bits and pieces of each other's interests and ideas. Laura grinned at the delight in Cass's face at each new acrobatic trick of the Chinese entertainers; Cass laughed at Laura's attempts to answer the questions of a large man in the colors of the Belarus team. Both happily snapped pictures of each other and other athletes, and occasionally signed memorabilia as it was handed to them.

Finally, the speeches were done and the *real* party began in earnest. Amidst a thunderous burst of pyrotechnics, China's hottest stars flew from the ceiling, popped from the floor and ran from the sides to begin the spectacle of entertainment to cap the evening. The international television coverage had stopped, leaving only the locals and the visiting competitors to revel the night away. This time was for the crowd, for the athletes, for the volunteers.

Cass found herself forced closer to Laura as the crowd behind them pressed toward the stage to be nearer to the singers. One surge of the crowd nearly knocked Cass from her feet; only Laura's quick reflexes and strong grip kept her from falling. Cass grinned at Laura and righted herself, glad to have someone bigger nearby in the growing crush. Another yell to the right, another singer, another shove and once again Cass lost her footing; once again, Laura reached out just in time. This time Laura did not let go.

"Here, hold onto me, I won't let you fall." Cass felt her hand engulfed by Laura's larger one and she smiled up at her. For a moment, as her eyes met Laura's, the music and laughter around them faded. They were jostled again and Laura tugged Cass a little closer, pulling her into the circle of her arms. She bent her head and put her lips near Cass's ear, her low voice making Cass shiver. "Turn around, I'll watch your back. It's getting a little crazy in here, eh?"

Cass could only nod as Laura's arms moved around her. *Oh God! This is so not happening, right? Shut up, Cass, and enjoy it. Tonight is not real, it's magic.*

But this time I believe in the magic.

She settled against Laura and tilted her head to see the stage. She was very aware that her head was resting just under Laura's chin, Laura's breasts pressed against her back... *Ooh, yeah, this is so not real.*

Together they enjoyed the show, although if pressed, she could not have said with certainty what they saw and heard. Cass closed her eyes and just absorbed it all. The laughter, chatter and singing around her were muted somehow by the soft buzz of Laura's humming vibrating through her body. She felt Laura, with her chin resting atop Cass's, tilt her head into Cass's and breathe in deeply from time to time and Cass shivered each time it happened.

With a mighty *bang* the singers and musicians stopped, the crowd seeming to lift them up with their triumphant roar. It was over. One last, tremendous flash of light, color and sound and that was it. The 2008 Olympic Games had ended. For one last time, the stadium was plunged into darkness as the crowd roared, stomped and clapped its approval for the show, the athletes and the venues.

It was over.

"No," she muttered under her breath.

"What?" Laura's chin left the top of Cass's head, and she bent her head to speak into Cass's ear. "Cass?"

Cass tightened her grip on Laura's hands where they lay tight across her abdomen and shook her head. She hadn't realized she'd spoken aloud. She felt like a child being asked to leave a birthday party. "I, um. I don't want it to be over." She leaned her head back against Laura's shoulder, staring at the darkened sky above and letting the joy of the crowd and the comforting sensation of Laura's arms around her carry her, imprinting the moment in her memory forever.

Laura leaned further, shifting Cass to one side but keeping her tucked within her arms. Slowly Cass turned her head to face Laura, letting the green eyes capture her, ground her. She gave Laura what she knew was a weak smile, hoping she hadn't sounded as wimpy as she'd felt. Laura deliberately lowered her head, until their lips were brushing. "It's not over, Cass. It's just beginning." Softly, she touched her lips to Cass's, hesitating for a moment, waiting for a response.

Oh my... Cass's mind emptied of everything but the feel of

Laura's lips against hers. Someone groaned and Cass couldn't be certain the sound had not come from her. She shifted and turned, pulling Laura to her, tangling her fingers in her vibrant curls. This was like nothing she'd ever felt before, this was *it.* Kissing Laura was more than Cass had imagined. She lost herself in it—the softness, the texture, the unrestrained thrill of the moment. She felt Laura pull her closer, vaguely aware of the crowd around them; a sense that completely left her at the first touch of Laura's tongue against her lips, asking for entry. That brief touch flashed through her from head to toe and she opened herself to Laura fully.

Hours, minutes, a lifetime passed. For just a moment, Cass could see her future...their future. Together. She couldn't say how she knew, but she *knew.*

In this moment, anything was possible.

The kiss ended slowly, wonderingly. Cass slid her arms around the solid strength of Laura's body and reveled in the feeling of belonging as Laura held her tight. Trembling, they clung to each other for security, for strength. They stood, pressed closely together, their breath mingling, their pulses unsteady.

Slowly, Cass leaned back to look up into Laura's face, watching as those green eyes opened again and seemed to light from within. She nodded, rubbing her nose to Laura's. "Yes, it *is* beginning."

Publications from
Bella Books, Inc.
Women. Books. Even Better Together.
P.O. Box 10543
Tallahassee, FL 32302
Phone: 800-729-4992
www.bellabooks.com

CALM BEFORE THE STORM by Peggy J. Herring. Colonel Marcel Robideaux doesn't tell and so far no one official has asked, but the amorous pursuit by Jordan McGowan has her worried for both her career and her honor.
978-0-9677753-1-9

THE WILD ONE by Lyn Denison. Rachel Weston is busy keeping home and head together after the death of her husband. Her kids need her and what she doesn't need is the confusion that Quinn Farrelly creates in her body and heart.
978-0-9677753-4-0

LESSONS IN MURDER by Claire McNab. There's a corpse in the school with a neat hole in the head and a Black & Decker drill alongside. Which teacher should Inspector Carol Ashton suspect? Unfortunately, the alluring Sybil Quade is at the top of the list. First in this highly lauded series.
978-1-931513-65-4

WHEN AN ECHO RETURNS by Linda Kay Silva. The bayou where Echo Branson found her sanity has been swept clean by a hurricane — or at least they thought. Then an evil washed up by the storm comes looking for them all, one-by-one. Second in series.
978-1-59493-225-0

DEADLY INTERSECTIONS by Ann Roberts. Everyone is lying, including her own father and her girlfriend. Leaving matters to the professionals is supposed to be easier! Third in series with *PAID IN FULL* and *WHITE OFFERINGS*.
978-1-59493-224-3

SUBSTITUTE FOR LOVE by Karin Kallmaker. No substitutes, ever again! But then Holly's heart, body and soul are captured by Reyna... Reyna with no last name and a secret life that hides a terrible bargain, one written in family blood.
978-1-931513-62-3

MAKING UP FOR LOST TIME by Karin Kallmaker. Take one Next Home Network Star and add one Little White Lie to equal mayhem in little Mendocino and a recipe for sizzling romance. This lighthearted, steamy story is a feast for the senses in a kitchen that is way too hot.
978-1-931513-61-6

2ND FIDDLE by Kate Calloway. Cassidy James's first case left her with a broken heart. At least this new case is fighting the good fight, and she can throw all her passion and energy into it.
978-1-59493-200-7

HUNTING THE WITCH by Ellen Hart. The woman she loves — used to love — offers her help, and Jane Lawless finds it hard to say no. She needs TLC for recent injuries and who better than a doctor? But Julia's jittery demeanor awakens Jane's curiosity. And Jane has never been able to resist a mystery. #9 in series and Lammy-winner.
978-1-59493-206-9

FAÇADES by Alex Marcoux. Everything Anastasia ever wanted — she has it. Sidney is the woman who helped her get it. But keeping it will require a price — the unnamed passion that simmers between them.
978-1-59493-239-7

ELENA UNDONE by Nicole Conn. The risks. The passion. The devastating choices. The ultimate rewards. Nicole Conn rocked the lesbian cinema world with Claire of the Moon and has rocked it again with Elena Undone. This is the book that tells it all...
978-1-59493-254-0

WHISPERS IN THE WIND by Frankie J. Jones. It began as a camping trip, then a simple hike. Dixon Hayes and Elizabeth Colter uncover an intriguing cave on their hike, changing their world, perhaps irrevocably.
978-1-59493-037-9

WEDDING BELL BLUES by Julia Watts. She'll do anything to save what's left of her family. Anything. It didn't seem like a bad plan...at first. Hailed by readers as Lammy-winner Julia Watts' funniest novel.
978-1-59493-199-4

WILDFIRE by Lynn James. From the moment botanist Devon McKinney meets ranger Elaine Thomas the chemistry is undeniable. Sharing — and protecting — a mountain for the length of their short assignments leads to unexpected passion in this sizzling romance by newcomer Lynn James.
978-1-59493-191-8

LEAVING L.A. by Kate Christie. Eleanor Chapin is on the way to the rest of her life when Tessa Flanaghan offers her a lucrative summer job caring for Tessa's daughter Laya. It's only temporary and everyone expects Eleanor to be leaving L.A...
978-1-59493-221-2

SOMETHING TO BELIEVE by Robbi McCoy. When Lauren and Cassie meet on a once-in-a-lifetime river journey through China their feelings are innocent...at first. Ten years later, nothing — and everything — has changed. From Golden Crown winner Robbi McCoy.
978-1-59493-214-4

DEVIL'S ROCK: THE SEARCH FOR PATRICK DOE by Gerri Hill. Deputy Andrea Sullivan and Agent Cameron Ross vow to bring a killer to justice. The killer has other plans. Gerri Hill pens another intriguing blend of mystery and romance in this page-turning thriller.
978-1-59493-218-2

SHADOW POINT by Amy Briant. Madison Maguire has just been not-quite fired, told her brother is dead and discovered she has to pick up a five-year old niece she's never met. After she makes it to Shadow Point it seems like someone—or something—doesn't want her to leave. Romance sizzles in this ghost story from Amy Briant.
978-1-59493-216-8

JUKEBOX by Gina Daggett. Debutantes in love. With each other. Two young women chafe at the constraints of parents and society with a friendship that could be more, if they can break free. Gina Daggett is best known as "Lipstick" of the columnist duo Lipstick & Dipstick.
978-1-59493-212-0

BLIND BET by Tracey Richardson. The stakes are high when Ellen Turcotte and Courtney Langford meet at the blackjack tables. Lady Luck has been smiling on Courtney but Ellen is a wild card she may not be able to handle.
978-1-59493-211-3